Pr

The sea has always been a place (ce
that has drawn explorers, adven   or
centuries. Its waves whisper of distant lands, uncharted territories, and ancient secrets buried beneath the depths. For those brave enough to venture into the unknown, the sea offers both the promise of glory and the threat of ruin.

This story is born from such a journey—a voyage undertaken with hope and ambition but shadowed by forces far greater than any man could have anticipated. What begins as a quest for discovery soon turns into a struggle for survival, as the crew of the *Santa Maria* faces not only the perils of the ocean but the ancient powers that have long ruled its waters. The island they stumble upon is not a new land to be claimed, but a realm forgotten by time, guarded by gods and creatures beyond human comprehension.

At its heart, this is a story of the cost of ambition, of the lengths to which men will go to conquer the unknown, and the dangerous line that is crossed when secrets meant to remain hidden are disturbed. It is about the weight of silence, the burden of keeping the truth buried, and the sacrifices made to protect the world from forces it is not ready to understand.

The legends of the sea are many—whispers of monsters, lost lands, and ancient civilizations long vanished beneath the waves. But some legends are more than mere stories. Some are warnings, carried by the wind and the tide, meant to keep us from straying too far into the abyss.

This is one such legend.

The men who survived this journey returned with their lives, but they also carried something far greater—knowledge of a place that should never be spoken of. They returned home, not with riches or glory, but with a vow of silence that would haunt them for the rest of their days.

1

And now, the sea waits, as it always has, for those who dare to seek its forbidden secrets.

But be warned—some secrets come at too great a cost.

The Abyss of Columbus: A Journey Beyond the Edge of the World

David Moore

Published by David Moore, 2024.

THE ABYSS OF COLUMBUS: A JOURNEY BEYOND THE EDGE OF THE WORLD

First edition. October 7, 2024.

Copyright © 2024 David Moore.

ISBN: 979-8227114020

Written by David Moore.

Table of Contents

To the dreamers and explorers, past and present, who dare to venture into the unknown. And to those who navigate the depths of their own fears, seeking light in the darkness.

Part I: The Call of the Ocean
Chapter 1: A Bold Venture

The grand hall of the Spanish court buzzed with excitement and skepticism. The air was thick with the scent of incense, and the chatter of nobles filled the space as Christopher Columbus strode purposefully toward the throne. Dressed in his finest yet weathered clothes, his eyes gleamed with conviction—a conviction that had carried him through years of rejection and scorn. Today, he hoped, that would all change.

Columbus stood before King Ferdinand and Queen Isabella, the two most powerful figures in all of Spain, and the people whose support he desperately needed to turn his dream into reality. His heart raced, but his voice remained steady. He presented his audacious plan to sail west, not into the perilous unknown, but toward the riches of the Indies. The Silk Road had grown treacherous, and the sea route around Africa seemed endless. But Columbus believed he could shorten the distance and change the course of history.

With a well-practiced tone, he spoke of adventure, of trade, and of the promise of gold and spices—treasures that would enrich the Spanish crown and secure their dominance over Portugal and other rising European powers. The court murmured, but the monarchs listened intently. Some nobles scoffed at the idea, whispering doubts about the existence of any land across the western horizon. The ocean, after all, was said to be a place of monsters and endless storms, a place from which no sailor returned.

But Columbus' confidence never wavered. He spoke with passion, describing the navigational techniques he had mastered and the stars that would guide his path. He promised glory and wealth, a new route to the Indies that would make Spain the envy of the world.

For a moment, the court fell silent, the weight of Columbus' words hanging in the air. Ferdinand and Isabella exchanged glances, their expressions unreadable. The queen, in particular, seemed to consider the boldness of the man before her. Was this truly a man of vision or just another dreamer bound for failure?

In that silence, Columbus knew that the fate of his journey—and perhaps the fate of the known world—hung in the balance.

Chapter 2: The Man Called Niño

The deck of the *Santa Maria* creaked under the weight of the crew's hurried preparations. It was still early in the morning, the sun barely peeking over the horizon, casting long shadows across the bustling port of Palos de la Frontera. Sailors moved about like ants, securing provisions, tying down rigging, and preparing for what would become the most significant voyage in human history. At the center of it all was a man whose quiet presence commanded more respect than any shouted order—the enigmatic navigator known only as Niño.

Juan Niño de La Rota, as his name was listed in the ship's records, was no stranger to the sea. His reputation had long preceded him among sailors and traders alike. Born in the coastal town of Moguer, his early life had been spent on fishing boats and merchant vessels, learning the intricate dance of the winds and tides. By the time he had reached manhood, he had already crossed the Mediterranean, navigated the treacherous currents of the North Atlantic, and traveled further south than any European dared, into the mysterious waters near the coast of Africa.

But it wasn't just Niño's skill that set him apart from the other men on Columbus' expedition. There was something else about him—something that both fascinated and unnerved those who worked alongside him. Whispers floated among the crew as they watched him move effortlessly through his tasks, his gaze always fixed on the horizon as if he could see beyond the limits of the known world.

Some said that Niño was not fully Spanish. His skin, darker than that of his countrymen, and his features, a blend of Iberian and something more exotic, fueled rumors. Some of the crew believed he had African blood, a connection to the great empires of Mali or the legendary land of Ethiopia, where kings and scholars had long mastered the art of seafaring. Others claimed he was descended from a line of Moorish navigators who had fled south after the Reconquista, taking with them ancient knowledge of the stars and oceans that had been passed down for generations.

Whatever the truth, Niño never spoke of his past. He remained a man of few words, his focus always on the sea and the ships that sailed it. To the men who worked under him, this reticence made him both a source of mystery and a figure of quiet authority. When he gave orders, they were followed without question. His calm demeanor and precise instructions could turn the most chaotic moments at sea into a well-coordinated dance of survival.

It was this reputation that had caught the attention of Christopher Columbus. After securing the blessing of the Spanish monarchs, Columbus had sought out the best navigators and sailors to man his fleet. He had heard tales of Niño's exploits and his ability to guide ships through the most dangerous of waters. Columbus, always a keen judge of character, had immediately recognized the value of having someone like Niño on his voyage. It was said that Niño could read the stars as easily as most men read books, and his knowledge of oceanic currents surpassed that of any other sailor Columbus had encountered.

Still, there were those aboard the *Santa Maria* who were uneasy about Niño's presence. Diego, a young cabin boy barely sixteen, had overheard a group of sailors whispering in the galley late one night. They spoke of Niño's uncanny ability to predict storms and navigate through fog as though he had some unholy pact with the ocean. One man swore that during a previous voyage with Niño, they had sailed through waters filled with ghostly lights—glowing, spectral beings just beneath the surface—only for Niño to calmly chart a course around them without so much as a glance at the sky.

"He's touched, that one," one of the sailors had muttered, shaking his head. "Not natural, I tell you. No man should know the sea like that."

Diego, wide-eyed and eager for adventure, had crept closer to the men, hoping to hear more. But as soon as Niño's name was mentioned again, the conversation died. One of the older sailors noticed Diego's presence and quickly sent him off with a warning glance. The boy had scampered away, his mind racing with the possibilities. Could the rumors be true? Was there something more to the man who now stood at the helm of their voyage?

The truth was, Niño's connection to the sea ran deeper than any of the men could understand. From a young age, he had been drawn to the ocean, its endless horizon calling to him in ways he could never fully explain. His mother, a healer from a small coastal village, had often spoken of the spirits of the water, beings that lived in the depths and whispered to those who listened closely enough. Niño had laughed it off as a child's tale, but as he grew older and spent more time on the water, he began to feel something—an intuition, perhaps—that guided him through even the darkest nights at sea.

His father, a trader who had once sailed as far south as the Gold Coast of Africa, had also left his mark on the boy. Niño had inherited his father's sharp mind for navigation and his thirst for exploration. But it was in the tales his father told of the African sailors—men who charted their courses not by the stars alone, but by the winds, the waves, and the very rhythm of the ocean—that Niño found his deepest inspiration.

In the years since his father's death, Niño had made it his mission to master these ancient techniques. He had sailed with Berber merchants, learned from Moorish scholars in Al-Andalus before their expulsion, and even ventured into the waters off the Canary Islands, where he had seen firsthand the remains of a great civilization swallowed by the sea.

Now, standing aboard the *Santa Maria*, Niño felt the familiar pull of the ocean beneath him. His dark eyes scanned the horizon as the ship began to drift away from the shore. He could sense the growing excitement among the men, the anticipation of adventure, but he knew better than to let his guard down. The sea was as fickle as it was beautiful, and in these uncharted waters, there were dangers far greater than any of them could imagine.

As the ship sailed west, Niño remained silent, his thoughts drifting back to the stories his mother had told. The spirits of the water. The forgotten gods of the deep. He had always believed them to be myths. But now, with the vast unknown stretching out before him, he began to wonder if there was more truth to those tales than he had ever allowed himself to believe.

And so, the man called Niño stood at the edge of the world, guiding Columbus and his crew into the abyss—where legends, and nightmares, waited.

Chapter 3: The Fleet Sets Sail

The morning sun cast a golden glow over the harbor at Palos de la Frontera as the three ships—*Santa Maria*, *Pinta*, and *Niña*—bobbed gently in the waters, their sails rustling in the light breeze. It was a momentous day, one that the people of the town would speak of for generations. The harbor was bustling with activity as sailors hurried to and fro, securing the final provisions, checking the rigging, and readying the ships for the long and uncertain voyage ahead. On the docks, families embraced their loved ones, offering prayers for safe passage. The air was thick with anticipation and a sense of history in the making.

Christopher Columbus stood aboard the *Santa Maria*, his flagship, surveying the scene. His heart swelled with pride and determination. This was the day he had been waiting for—years of planning, pleading, and perseverance had led to this moment. Behind him stood the crew, a mix of seasoned sailors, young adventurers, and a few who had joined the voyage out of desperation. All eyes were on him, and he knew that in this moment, they needed his confidence to bolster their own.

Columbus stepped forward, raising his hand to quiet the murmurs of the men. "Today, we embark on a journey that will change the course of history," he began, his voice strong and steady. "We sail not just for glory or for riches, but for the future of Spain and the world. We will find the Indies by sailing west, and when we return, we will return as heroes!"

The crew erupted in cheers, their excitement palpable. The promise of untold wealth and adventure was enough to ignite their spirits, even though the dangers that lay ahead were still unknown to them. They believed in Columbus—or at least, they wanted to believe in him. After all, what choice did they have now that the sails were raised and the ropes unfastened?

As Columbus continued to speak, another figure stood quietly at the bow of the *Santa Maria*, watching the horizon. Juan Niño de La Rota, the fleet's lead navigator, had a far more subdued expression. He listened to Columbus' rousing speech, but his eyes never left the distant sky, where dark clouds were beginning to gather. A slight unease crept into his mind, a nagging sense that the sea was not as welcoming as the crew imagined.

Niño had been at sea for most of his life, and he knew the signs when the ocean was about to turn. The breeze, though soft now, carried a certain weight—a dampness that foretold the coming of rain. He could feel the tension in the air, the way the waves began to tug ever so slightly against the hull. But he remained silent. There was no need to spoil the high spirits of the men just yet. They would learn soon enough that the sea was not to be trifled with.

The sails of the *Santa Maria* unfurled, catching the wind in their broad canvas. The ship lurched forward, gliding gracefully away from the dock. The *Pinta* and *Niña* followed suit, their crews working in unison to guide the ships out of the harbor. Cheers erupted from the townspeople who had gathered to watch the fleet's departure. The sound of horns and drums echoed across the water, a festive send-off for the brave souls heading into the unknown.

As the ships left the safety of the harbor and began their journey into the open sea, the mood aboard the vessels remained jubilant. The sailors sang sea shanties, their voices rising over the wind as they worked the ropes and rigging. Some of the younger men exchanged excited glances, eager for the adventure that awaited them beyond the horizon. To them, this was the start of something grand, something to be remembered for all time.

But for Columbus and Niño, there was a different weight to this voyage. Columbus, standing at the helm, felt the immense pressure of his ambition. He had staked everything—his reputation, his future—on this journey. Failure was not an option. The monarchs had given him their trust, and now he had to deliver. His mind buzzed with thoughts of distant lands and riches yet unseen. He had no doubt in his mind that they would find the Indies, and that Spain would be forever grateful for his vision.

Niño, however, was less concerned with riches or fame. His focus was on the sea and the ships under his care. He knew the ocean's moods better than any man aboard, and something in the wind told him that this journey would not be as smooth as many hoped. The clouds on the horizon were no mere passing storm. Niño sensed something darker, something more ominous brewing in the depths of the ocean—an unease that went beyond natural phenomena.

As the hours passed and the fleet sailed further from the coast, the sky began to change. The bright blue of morning gave way to a dull gray, and the wind picked up, tugging harder at the sails. The crew, still high-spirited, began to notice the shift, but they brushed it off. A little storm was to be expected—they were sailors, after all. What was the sea without a few rough days?

But Niño knew better. He moved to Columbus' side, his voice low and steady as he spoke. "The wind is changing. We may be in for more than just a simple storm."

Columbus glanced at the sky, his expression unreadable. "We've sailed through storms before," he replied, his voice firm. "This one will pass, as they always do."

Niño didn't argue, but his eyes remained fixed on the clouds. There was something unnatural about the way they moved, swirling in dark, thick masses that seemed to defy the usual patterns of the sky. He had heard tales of strange storms, tempests that came out of nowhere, swallowing ships whole. They were the kinds of stories told late at night around campfires, the kind that sent chills down a sailor's spine. But Niño had never believed in such things—until now.

The first drops of rain began to fall, light at first, barely noticeable against the wind. But within minutes, the rain intensified, slamming against the deck with a ferocity that sent men scrambling for cover. The wind howled, tugging at the sails and whipping the ropes like wild serpents. Columbus barked orders, his voice rising above the storm as he directed the crew to secure the ship.

Niño moved quickly, his hands steady as he adjusted the course. The sea had turned against them, the waves rising higher with each passing moment. The *Santa Maria* groaned as it was tossed by the swelling waters, and the other ships struggled to keep up.

As the storm raged, the men fought to control the ship, their earlier enthusiasm now replaced with grim determination. The once-lively songs of the crew were drowned out by the roaring wind and crashing waves.

This was no ordinary storm. The fleet had barely begun its journey, and already the sea had shown its teeth. But Niño knew, deep in his bones, that this was only the beginning. Darker forces were at play, and they were heading straight into the heart of it.

The fleet sailed on, battered but intact, into the unknown. The storm clouds loomed larger, a harbinger of the challenges yet to come.

Chapter 4: Whispers of the Unknown

The storm that had assaulted the fleet on their first day at sea had finally abated, leaving behind a bruised sky and choppy waves. The *Santa Maria*, *Pinta*, and *Niña* pressed onward, their sails patched and ropes re-secured. The atmosphere aboard the ships, however, had shifted dramatically. The lively spirit that had once filled the decks was replaced with an uneasy silence. As the fleet sailed further from the familiar shores of Spain, the vastness of the open ocean stretched out endlessly before them, and with it, the men's fears grew.

At first, the crew attributed the growing sense of dread to the storm. After all, storms at sea were not uncommon, and they had survived this one with only minor damage. But as the days passed and the coastline disappeared into memory, whispers began to circulate among the men—whispers of strange sights and sounds in the deep, of unnatural forces that lived far beyond the reach of any land.

It started with one of the younger sailors aboard the *Pinta*. Late one night, while most of the crew slept, he had been keeping watch near the bow of the ship. The sky was clear, the stars shining brightly above, when he noticed something strange below the surface of the water. At first, he thought it was a trick of the moonlight, the way the waves moved and shimmered in the dark. But as he leaned closer, he saw them—glowing shapes, just beneath the surface, moving in rhythm with the ship.

He called out to another sailor, but by the time they returned, the lights had vanished. Dismissed as an overactive imagination, the story was quickly forgotten by the officers, but it took root among the crew. The younger men, especially, were eager to share the tale, embellishing it as it passed from mouth to mouth.

"They say it's the souls of drowned sailors," one man muttered, his voice barely audible over the creaking of the ship's timbers. "Lost to the depths, cursed to follow any ship that sails too far into their waters."

"Nonsense," another scoffed, though his voice wavered. "It was probably a school of fish, nothing more."

But the fear was contagious. Sailors who had once laughed off the idea of dangers lurking in the deep now found themselves avoiding the edges of the deck at night, unwilling to look too closely at the water below.

Niño, ever the watchful navigator, overheard the rumors but remained silent. He had seen the fear growing in the men's eyes, felt the tension that crackled through the air like an unspoken curse. Though he didn't give in to the wild tales of glowing spirits, he couldn't deny that something felt different out here. The further they sailed, the more he sensed a shift, as though the ocean itself was watching them.

It wasn't long before other strange occurrences began to fuel the crew's anxieties. One morning, the crew of the *Niña* awoke to find that several ropes had been severed during the night. There had been no storm, no strong winds to account for the damage, and the cuts were clean, almost as if made by a blade. Some of the men whispered of sea demons with sharp teeth, creatures that lurked beneath the waves and attacked ships in the dead of night.

Another night, aboard the *Santa Maria*, a sailor named Rodrigo claimed to have seen something far worse. He had been on the night watch, the only one awake save for Niño, who was taking his usual turn at the helm. As the ship glided through the dark water, Rodrigo swore he saw something large rise from the depths, a dark shape that towered above the ship for just a moment before sinking back into the ocean. He described it as a massive, shadowy figure with eyes that glowed like embers in the night. No one else had seen it, and the story was met with skepticism, but it was enough to ignite more fears among the crew.

Niño had heard similar tales in his youth—stories told by the elders of coastal villages who warned of the creatures that lived beyond the known seas. They spoke of ancient beings that ruled the waters long before men had ever set sail, beings that could control the tides and summon storms at will. He had dismissed those tales as legends, mere folklore meant to scare children away from the dangerous shores. But now, far from the safety of land, he began to wonder if there was some truth to those old stories.

As the days passed, the tension aboard the ships grew thicker. Men who had once been bold and adventurous now kept to themselves, speaking in hushed tones and avoiding the dark waters as if they feared what might be lurking just below the surface. Even Columbus noticed the change in morale, though he tried to dismiss it as the natural wear of being at sea for so long.

One evening, as the sun sank below the horizon and the world was cast in shades of red and gold, Columbus gathered his officers for a meeting in his quarters. Niño, standing quietly by the window, listened as Columbus addressed their concerns.

"We must maintain order," Columbus said, his voice firm. "The men are restless, but we cannot afford to let these wild rumors take hold. There is nothing out there but the ocean and our destination. We will reach the Indies, and when we do, these foolish fears will be forgotten."

The officers nodded, though their expressions were uncertain. They had heard the rumors too, and though they didn't believe in sea monsters or spirits, they could not deny the strange events that had occurred since the storm. Still, they trusted Columbus, and more importantly, they knew they had no choice but to continue forward. Turning back now would be seen as a failure, and none of them were willing to return to Spain empty-handed.

After the meeting, Niño lingered, his eyes fixed on the horizon. The sun had set, and the first stars of the night twinkled in the sky. He could feel the weight of the ocean beneath them, its vastness pressing down on the ships like an unseen force. Something was out there—of that much, he was certain. But whether it was a force of nature or something far older and darker, he did not yet know.

As the night deepened and the ships sailed further into the unknown, the whispers among the crew grew louder. Every creak of the ship, every shadow that passed beneath the water, fed their fears. They had set sail for the Indies, but as the days dragged on, the men began to wonder if they had ventured into a place far stranger—a place where the laws of the known world no longer applied.

Niño stood alone on the deck, his eyes scanning the horizon for signs of land, but there was only the endless sea. In the silence, he thought he could hear it—the faintest whisper, carried on the wind. Something ancient. Something watching.

And so, the fleet sailed on, deeper into the unknown, as the whispers of danger grew louder with each passing day.

Part II: Into the Abyss
Chapter 5: Days Without Land

The sun rose and set in an endless, monotonous cycle as the days bled into weeks with no land in sight. The excitement that had filled the crew at the start of the journey had long since dissipated, replaced by an uneasy restlessness. Every morning, the men woke with the hope that the horizon would finally reveal the shores of the Indies, and every evening they went to sleep with growing doubts gnawing at their minds. The vast, empty ocean seemed to stretch forever in all directions, offering no sign that they were anywhere close to their intended destination.

At first, the men had taken comfort in Columbus' unwavering confidence. He stood tall at the helm of the *Santa Maria*, scanning the horizon with the same determination he had shown from the beginning. But as days turned into weeks, and the provisions began to dwindle, even Columbus' optimism could not quell the rising fear among the crew. The wind, once their greatest ally, now seemed a cruel reminder of the endless journey ahead, propelling them deeper into the unknown with no promise of an end in sight.

The murmurs of doubt, which had begun as quiet whispers below deck, grew louder with each passing day. The men were growing impatient, their trust in Columbus wearing thin. They had believed in his vision of reaching the Indies by sailing west, but now that hope was fading, replaced by a creeping suspicion that perhaps they had been led astray. Perhaps there was no land beyond the horizon—only an endless expanse of water, stretching on forever.

"I'm telling you," one of the sailors muttered to his companion as they worked to secure the sails, "we're never going to find land. We've been out here for weeks, and what have we seen? Nothing but water and sky."

His companion, a burly man with weathered hands, nodded grimly. "I heard some of the men talking last night. They say Columbus doesn't know where he's going. That he's leading us all to our deaths."

The first sailor glanced nervously over his shoulder before lowering his voice even further. "There's talk of turning back. Some of the men are saying we should head for Spain while we still can. Better to return empty-handed than to die out here in the middle of nowhere."

The other man grunted in agreement, but neither of them dared say more. The thought of mutiny, though tempting, was dangerous. Columbus had powerful backers in the Spanish court, and the consequences of disobedience would be severe. Still, the idea lingered in the minds of the crew as they went about their tasks, their eyes constantly flicking toward the horizon, hoping for a sign that their journey had not been in vain.

Meanwhile, Niño, the fleet's enigmatic navigator, remained a calm presence amid the growing unrest. While the others fretted and whispered, Niño kept his focus on the stars and the sky, trusting in the ancient navigational techniques he had learned over the years. He was not a man given to panic or doubt, and he knew better than most that the ocean was an unpredictable beast. Journeys like this were never straightforward, and the sea often tested those who ventured into its depths. But Niño had a quiet faith in the stars, and he continued to guide the fleet westward, confident that they were on the right course.

He had learned to read the skies like an old friend, understanding the subtle shifts in the winds and the patterns of the clouds. At night, he would spend hours studying the constellations, marking their positions and comparing them to the charts he had memorized long ago. The stars had never led him astray before, and though the journey had taken longer than expected, Niño remained convinced that land was out there, waiting to be found.

Columbus often came to Niño for reassurance, his own confidence beginning to waver as the days dragged on. One evening, as the sun sank below the horizon and the sky turned a deep shade of violet, Columbus approached him on the deck.

"What do you think, Niño?" Columbus asked, his voice low so that the other men wouldn't hear the doubt creeping into his tone. "Are we still on the right path?"

Niño glanced at the horizon, where the last rays of sunlight were disappearing into the ocean. He nodded slowly, his gaze steady. "We are, Admiral. The stars tell me we are heading in the right direction."

Columbus exhaled, relieved by Niño's calm certainty. "The men are growing restless," he admitted, his eyes dark with concern. "They're starting to lose faith in the voyage."

Niño's expression remained impassive. "They are afraid, as all men are when faced with the unknown. But fear is a poor guide, and it will only lead them to ruin. We must stay the course."

Columbus nodded, though the weight of the crew's mounting discontent hung heavily on his shoulders. He knew that morale was slipping, and it wouldn't be long before the whispers of mutiny became more than just talk. But for now, he trusted Niño's judgment. The navigator had proven himself time and time again, guiding the fleet through storms and keeping them on track. If Niño believed they were on the right path, then Columbus would trust him—at least for a little while longer.

But the rest of the crew did not share Columbus' faith. As the days stretched into weeks, the men grew more and more agitated. Arguments broke out over small things—who was responsible for certain duties, how much food was being rationed, and who had seen what in the water. The once-disciplined sailors now snapped at each other, their tempers flaring with increasing frequency.

Diego, the young cabin boy, had overheard several conversations between the older sailors. He had seen the looks of doubt in their eyes, the way they muttered under their breath whenever Columbus passed by. The atmosphere on the ship was tense, like a rope pulled too tight, ready to snap at any moment.

One evening, as the ships sailed through a calm, eerily still sea, a group of men gathered in the galley of the *Santa Maria*. Their faces were shadowed, their voices low as they discussed what should be done.

"We can't keep going like this," one of the men, a burly sailor named Vicente, said, slamming his fist on the table. "Columbus is leading us to our deaths. We need to turn back before it's too late."

"But what if we're close?" another man countered, his voice uncertain. "What if we're only a few days from land?"

Vicente shook his head. "How many days have we been saying that? Weeks? We've seen nothing but water. I don't know about you, but I'm not about to die out here waiting for a miracle that isn't coming."

There were murmurs of agreement around the table. The men's faces were hard, their eyes filled with fear and frustration. They had put their faith in Columbus, but now that faith was crumbling under the weight of the endless ocean and the nagging sense that they had ventured too far.

As the crew continued to debate, Niño stood alone at the helm, his eyes scanning the sky. The stars shone brightly above, as they always had, guiding him through the dark expanse of the ocean. He knew that the men's doubts were growing, but he also knew that they were close—closer than any of them realized.

The ocean was a patient, fickle mistress, and she often tested those who sought to conquer her. But Niño had faith in the stars, in the ancient knowledge passed down through generations of navigators. He would guide them to land, even if it was the last thing he did.

The question was, would the crew hold out long enough to see it?

Chapter 6: The Tempest

The sky had taken on an ominous hue, a sickly green-gray that seemed to churn with the gathering fury of the heavens. It was late afternoon, and the usual quiet murmur of the crew had grown uneasy. The wind, once a steady, comforting force driving the ships westward, had become erratic, gusting wildly one moment and dying down the next. The clouds, thick and low, swirled together as if they were conspiring against the fleet.

Columbus stood at the helm of the *Santa Maria*, his eyes narrowed as he watched the sky darken further. He had seen storms before, of course, but something about this one unsettled him. It felt... different, as though the sea itself was preparing to unleash its wrath. His gut told him that this would be no ordinary squall, and the knots in his stomach tightened with each gust of wind.

Niño, however, remained calm. As the wind picked up and the first drops of rain splattered against the deck, he silently adjusted the sails, his movements precise and measured. His eyes scanned the horizon, reading the clouds and the currents with the practiced ease of a man who had spent his life on the water. He could feel the storm brewing, but he also knew that panic would only make things worse.

"Prepare the men," Niño said quietly to Columbus, his voice steady despite the rising wind. "It's coming fast."

Columbus nodded, then turned to bark orders at the crew. "All hands on deck! Secure the lines, reef the sails! Prepare for a storm!"

The men scrambled into action, tying down everything that could be lashed, securing barrels, and battening down the hatches. The *Santa Maria* groaned as the waves began to swell, lifting the ship higher and higher before crashing back down with a violent force. The *Pinta* and *Niña*, trailing behind, could be seen struggling to maintain their course, their masts swaying dangerously with each new wave.

Within minutes, the sky had gone completely dark, as though night had fallen prematurely. The rain came down in torrents, driven sideways by the howling wind, and the sea itself seemed to rise up in anger. Massive waves pounded the sides of the ships, sending water cascading over the decks. The sailors clung to the rigging and each other, fighting to keep their footing as the ships were tossed like toys in a tempest.

Lightning slashed through the sky, illuminating the chaos in brief, terrifying flashes. Each bolt seemed to strike closer than the last, lighting up the faces of the men as they fought against the storm. Thunder followed, so loud it felt like the sky itself was cracking open. The storm's fury was unlike anything they had ever encountered, and for a moment, even the most seasoned sailors wondered if they were sailing into the very heart of the ocean's wrath.

Amid the chaos, Niño moved with calm precision. While the crew battled the elements, he focused on keeping the *Santa Maria* on course, his hands steady on the helm. His years of experience told him that fighting the storm head-on would only lead to disaster. The key was to work with the wind and the waves, to guide the ship through the storm's path rather than resist it.

"The winds are shifting!" he called out over the roar of the storm. "We need to adjust the sails. Keep her steady—if we turn too sharply, we'll capsize."

The men strained to hear him over the storm's fury, but his authority was unmistakable. Even Columbus, who was usually the one giving orders, had fallen silent, trusting Niño's judgment in this life-or-death moment.

As Niño expertly navigated through the rising swell, the ship pitched and rolled violently. Several men were thrown off their feet, and one sailor nearly went overboard before another grabbed him by the wrist and pulled him back from the brink. The sea lashed at them, its cold, salty spray stinging their eyes and soaking their clothes. Every wave felt like it might be the one to break the ship in half, yet somehow, under Niño's guidance, the *Santa Maria* held firm.

The storm seemed to go on forever. Time lost all meaning as the men fought to keep the ship from being swallowed by the ocean. Hours passed in a blur of wind, water, and fear. The *Pinta* and *Niña* were barely visible now, their lights flickering like tiny candles in the distance, constantly being extinguished by the driving rain. Every time the ships disappeared behind a wave, the crew held their breath, wondering if they would ever reappear.

"Hold steady!" Niño shouted, his voice barely audible above the storm's roar. He knew that the worst of it was still to come. The wind was swirling in strange, unnatural patterns, and the waves were becoming more unpredictable. They were in the heart of the storm now, surrounded by its fury on all sides.

Suddenly, a massive wave, larger than any that had come before, rose up in front of the *Santa Maria*, towering over the ship like a wall of dark, churning water. The men froze, staring in terror as the wave surged toward them. It seemed impossible that the ship could survive such a force.

Niño acted quickly, yanking the wheel hard to the right. The ship groaned in protest, its timbers creaking under the strain, but it turned just in time. The wave slammed into the side of the ship, sending water crashing over the deck and nearly tipping the vessel on its side. Men were thrown against the rails, clinging desperately to anything they could grab, but somehow, miraculously, the ship stayed afloat.

Columbus, soaked and shaken, looked at Niño with wide eyes. "How...?" he began, but he didn't need to finish the question. Niño's calm, quiet competence had saved them from certain destruction.

"We have to keep moving," Niño said, his voice steady but grim. "If we stop now, the next wave will take us for sure."

And so, the crew fought on. The storm seemed endless, wave after wave crashing down on the ship as the wind howled like a living thing.

But Niño never wavered, guiding the *Santa Maria* with the precision of a man born to the sea. He felt the ship's every movement, adjusting their course with each new threat, navigating them through the storm's deadly grip.

Finally, after what felt like an eternity, the wind began to die down. The waves, while still powerful, no longer seemed intent on destroying the ship. The rain eased to a drizzle, and the dark clouds that had swallowed the sky began to break apart, revealing patches of starlit sky above.

The men, exhausted and soaked to the bone, collapsed where they stood, their bodies bruised and aching from the battle they had just endured. Many of them had thought they wouldn't survive the night, but somehow, against all odds, they had.

Columbus turned to Niño, his expression a mix of gratitude and disbelief. "You saved us."

Niño said nothing, merely nodding as he looked out over the now-quiet sea. The storm had passed, but something told him that the ocean's trials were far from over. For now, though, the ships remained afloat, and the journey continued.

As the crew began to recover, Niño turned his gaze once more to the horizon. There was no sign of land yet, but he knew it was out there, somewhere beyond the endless sea. And with the storm behind them, they were one step closer to finding it.

Chapter 7: Sea Serpents of the Deep

The morning after the storm was eerily calm. The sea, which had raged only hours before, was now as smooth as glass, reflecting the pale blue sky overhead. The ships—*Santa Maria*, *Pinta*, and *Niña*—were battered but intact, their sails still drying from the storm's relentless rain. The crew, exhausted and worn from the battle with the tempest, moved slowly about their duties, some still shaken by the violent ordeal they had survived.

Niño stood at the bow of the *Santa Maria*, his eyes scanning the horizon. The ocean stretched out in every direction, an endless expanse of water and sky. The storm had driven them far off course, but Niño, with his uncanny ability to navigate even the most treacherous of waters, was certain they were still headed west. He had guided them through the storm's fury, and now, they were once again chasing the promise of land.

But something wasn't right. As Niño gazed out over the calm waters, a sense of unease settled over him. The sea had grown unnaturally still, as if the storm had drawn away every trace of life from the ocean. No fish swam near the surface, no birds flew overhead. It was as though the storm had wiped the slate clean, leaving behind a desolate silence.

It wasn't long before the crew noticed it too. The men, who had been busy repairing the damage from the storm, began to whisper among themselves. The absence of sea life was unnerving, especially to the seasoned sailors who were accustomed to the constant presence of dolphins, seabirds, and the occasional school of fish. Now, there was nothing but the sound of creaking wood and the soft lapping of the waves against the hull.

As the sun climbed higher in the sky, the oppressive silence weighed heavier on the crew. They went about their work, but their eyes constantly flicked toward the water, searching for any sign of life.

Some of the men spoke in hushed tones about the strange occurrences that had plagued their journey so far—the storm, the whispers, the unsettling calm. But even those whispers were silenced when the first sailor spotted something in the water.

It was just after noon when the cry went up from the lookout atop the *Santa Maria*'s mast. "Something in the water!" he shouted, his voice trembling with excitement—or was it fear?

The crew scrambled to the rails, peering over the side of the ship. At first, they saw nothing but the calm, shimmering surface of the sea. But then, just beneath the water, something moved. It was subtle, a shadow gliding through the depths, but it was there—something large, something alive.

"Do you see it?" one of the sailors asked, his voice barely above a whisper.

"Aye," another replied, his eyes wide. "What is it?"

The shadow moved again, closer this time, and more men gathered at the rail, staring down into the water. The shape beneath the surface was massive, far larger than any fish or whale they had ever seen. It glided effortlessly through the water, its long, serpentine body undulating as it moved. And then, as the men watched in stunned silence, it rose closer to the surface, revealing a flash of scaly, black-green skin and a pair of glowing eyes that gleamed with an unnatural light.

Panic swept through the crew like wildfire. Shouts erupted from every corner of the ship as men scrambled away from the rail, their faces pale with fear. Whatever this creature was, it was no ordinary sea animal. It was something out of the sailors' worst nightmares, a monster from the stories they had heard as children—stories of creatures that lurked in the deepest parts of the ocean, waiting to drag ships down to the watery depths.

"What in God's name is that?" one of the men cried, his voice high with terror.

Niño stepped forward, his expression grim as he looked down at the creature. He had heard of such things before, in the old tales told by African and Moorish sailors who had ventured further south than any European. They spoke of sea serpents—massive, intelligent creatures that ruled the deep waters, rarely seen by men but always feared. He had dismissed those stories as myths, but now, staring down at the serpent below, he began to wonder if there had been truth in the legends after all.

The creature moved alongside the ship, its massive body coiling and uncoiling as it followed their course. Its glowing eyes seemed to fix on the ship, watching, waiting. And it wasn't alone. As the men gathered their wits and looked out over the water, they saw more shadows rising beneath the surface. There were at least three of them now, their long bodies snaking through the water, trailing the ships like silent predators.

"They're following us," one of the sailors said, his voice shaking. "Why are they following us?"

Columbus, who had been watching from the helm, strode toward Niño, his face pale but determined. "What do we do?" he asked, keeping his voice low so as not to spread more panic among the men.

Niño's brow furrowed as he considered their options. He had never faced creatures like this before, but he knew one thing: panic would only make things worse. The sea serpents were massive, and while they hadn't attacked, their presence alone was enough to unnerve even the bravest sailor. If they panicked, if they made a wrong move, it could provoke the creatures into attacking—and there was no telling what such monsters could do to their ships.

"Keep the men calm," Niño said quietly. "They're watching us, but they haven't attacked. We stay the course and act as though nothing is wrong. If we panic, they'll sense it."

Columbus nodded, though his jaw was tight with worry. "You think they'll let us pass?"

"I don't know," Niño admitted, his eyes never leaving the serpents. "But we have no other choice."

The crew, despite their fear, obeyed the orders to remain calm. But it was easier said than done. The sea serpents continued to follow the ships, their glowing eyes and massive bodies never far from view. Every now and then, one of them would breach the surface, its head rising briefly out of the water before slipping back below, sending waves crashing against the side of the ship.

As the hours passed, the tension on board became unbearable. Every creak of the wood, every splash of the waves, seemed to echo with the threat of the serpents below. The men worked in silence, their eyes constantly darting to the water, waiting for the creatures to make their move.

It was late in the afternoon when the creatures finally began to drift away. One by one, the serpents sank back into the depths, their glowing eyes disappearing beneath the surface until the water was still once more. The crew watched in stunned silence as the last of the shadows faded from view, leaving the ships alone once again on the vast, empty sea.

For a moment, no one spoke. Then, slowly, the men began to breathe again, their tense shoulders relaxing as the immediate danger passed. But the fear remained. The sea was no longer just a vast, empty expanse of water. It was alive, filled with creatures that defied explanation and threatened their very survival.

Columbus turned to Niño, his face pale but relieved. "What were they?"

Niño shook his head. "I don't know. But they were watching us. Waiting for something."

The crew, shaken but grateful to be alive, returned to their duties, though the fear lingered in their hearts. They had survived the storm, but now they knew that the ocean held dangers far greater than any tempest. And as the ships sailed on into the unknown, Niño kept his eyes on the horizon, knowing that this was only the beginning of the trials that awaited them.

Chapter 8: The First Attack

The calm that followed the appearance of the sea serpents was short-lived. Though the serpents had seemingly retreated into the depths, their presence weighed heavily on the minds of the men aboard the fleet. The brief respite gave them little solace, as the unnerving memory of the creatures' glowing eyes and enormous, undulating bodies lingered. The men of the *Santa Maria*, *Pinta*, and *Niña* worked tirelessly to repair the damage left by the storm, but now they moved with a sense of foreboding, always glancing at the water's surface, waiting for the next threat to emerge.

For a day and a night, the sea remained deceptively calm. The fleet continued its westward journey, cutting through the placid waters with an eerie sense of isolation. But the crew could not shake the feeling that they were being followed, hunted by something lurking just beneath the surface. They didn't speak of it openly, but every man felt it—the oppressive weight of eyes upon them.

It wasn't long before their worst fears materialized.

It was late afternoon when the attack came. The sky had turned a pale shade of pink, the sun dipping low on the horizon, casting long shadows over the water. The men of the *Pinta* had been working on reinforcing the hull when the first violent jolt rocked the ship.

The impact came without warning—a sickening crunch of wood splintering, followed by shouts of alarm. The *Pinta* lurched to the side as though something immense had slammed into it from below, throwing sailors off their feet and sending barrels and supplies tumbling across the deck.

"Something hit us!" one of the men yelled, scrambling to his feet as the ship listed dangerously to one side.

A second jolt struck, harder than the first, and this time there was no doubt about the cause. The *Pinta*'s hull groaned in protest as the wood splintered further, water beginning to rush in through the damaged planks. The crew rushed to the side of the ship, peering over the edge in time to see something enormous and serpentine vanish beneath the waves, its long, sinuous body gliding out of view.

"The creatures," one of the sailors gasped, his face pale with fear. "They're attacking!"

Panic erupted across the *Pinta* as the crew realized the gravity of their situation. The sea serpents, the very same creatures that had followed them so ominously before, were now attacking with full force. The men scrambled to action, shouting orders and grabbing tools to try and repair the damage to the hull. But the beasts were relentless.

A third jolt rocked the *Pinta*, this time sending a shower of seawater over the deck as the creature's massive body struck the ship again. The men could see it now—its thick, scaly tail whipping through the water as it circled the ship like a predator stalking its prey. The creature's head breached the surface for a moment, revealing glowing, malevolent eyes and a maw filled with razor-sharp teeth before it dove back beneath the waves.

"They're going to tear us apart!" one of the sailors screamed, his voice rising in terror.

Meanwhile, aboard the *Santa Maria*, Columbus and Niño watched in horror as the *Pinta* struggled against the assault. From their vantage point, they could see the serpent's massive body coil around the *Pinta*, the water churning violently as it thrashed against the ship.

"Get to the boats! We need to help them!" Columbus barked, rallying his crew to action.

Niño remained calm, his mind racing as he tried to think of a way to fight the creatures. The beasts were unlike anything he had ever encountered, and their strength was terrifying. But he knew that panic would only lead to more chaos. The key was to keep the ships afloat and buy enough time for the crew to fight back.

"Send men to reinforce the hull," Niño said, his voice steady despite the urgency of the situation. "If we can hold the ship together, we might be able to scare the creature off."

The *Santa Maria* crew hurried into action, preparing lifeboats and gathering supplies to send to the *Pinta*. But the water between the ships was treacherous, churned by the sea serpent's violent movements. The *Pinta* was listing dangerously now, water pouring in through the damaged hull faster than the men could patch it. Some of the sailors were already grabbing makeshift weapons—harpoons, knives, anything they could find to defend themselves.

Another violent impact rocked the *Pinta*, and this time the serpent's head reared out of the water, its glowing eyes locked onto the ship. It struck again, its massive tail slamming against the hull with enough force to send another deep crack through the planks. The men on deck shouted in panic as the creature's mouth opened, revealing rows of jagged teeth. One of the sailors, in a desperate act of defiance, hurled a spear at the beast, striking its scaly hide but causing little more than a shallow cut.

The serpent let out a deafening roar, its fury now fully unleashed. It lashed out again, its tail sweeping across the deck and knocking several men off their feet. One sailor was thrown overboard, disappearing into the water with a scream as the serpent dove after him, the water boiling in its wake.

Aboard the *Santa Maria*, the crew watched in horror as the attack escalated. Niño, still calm in the face of the chaos, signaled to the men in the lifeboats to hold back.

"We need to distract it," Niño muttered to Columbus, his mind working quickly. "If it focuses on us, the *Pinta* may have a chance to stabilize."

Columbus nodded, his jaw set in determination. "Do whatever it takes."

Niño moved swiftly, ordering the men to load the cannons on the *Santa Maria*. He knew that their small guns were no match for a creature of this size, but if they could create enough noise and confusion, they might be able to lure the serpent away from the *Pinta* long enough for the crew to make emergency repairs.

The cannons fired, the thunderous sound echoing across the water. The sea serpent, startled by the sudden noise, lifted its head and turned toward the *Santa Maria*. For a brief moment, the assault on the *Pinta* paused as the creature's attention shifted.

"Now!" Niño shouted. "Get to the *Pinta*! Help them reinforce the hull while we keep it distracted."

Several small boats from the *Santa Maria* and *Niña* raced across the water, carrying men armed with planks, hammers, and whatever tools they could gather. As the boats neared the *Pinta*, the serpent lashed out again, its massive tail slamming into the side of the ship, but the repairs had already begun.

The creature, enraged by the cannon fire, turned fully toward the *Santa Maria* and began to swim toward it, its enormous body cutting through the water with terrifying speed. Niño, his face calm but his heart pounding, gave the order to fire again. The second round of cannon shots splashed into the water around the serpent, sending up huge sprays but causing no real damage.

"Keep firing," Niño called. "We just need to hold it off long enough."

As the crew worked to distract the serpent, the men aboard the *Pinta* fought desperately to save their ship. The hull had been badly damaged, but they were making progress, sealing the cracks and reinforcing the planks as best they could.

After what felt like hours, the creature let out one final, ear-splitting roar before diving deep beneath the waves. The water calmed, the ripples fading as the serpent disappeared into the depths, leaving the fleet battered but alive.

The men aboard the *Pinta* sagged in relief, their bodies aching from the effort and terror. The ship was damaged but still afloat, and for now, the danger seemed to have passed.

But Niño knew better. As he watched the still surface of the water, he could feel it in his bones. The sea serpents weren't gone. They were waiting. Watching. And next time, they might not leave so easily.

Chapter 9: Niño's Secrets

The sea had calmed after the attack, but the atmosphere aboard the fleet remained tense. The men of the *Pinta* worked tirelessly to repair the damage inflicted by the sea serpent, their faces pale and drawn from the fear that still gripped them. Though the creature had vanished, it left behind a sense of dread that seemed to hang over the ships like a thick fog.

Columbus stood at the helm of the *Santa Maria*, his eyes scanning the horizon. The attack had shaken him more than he cared to admit. These waters were far more dangerous than he had anticipated, filled with creatures and phenomena that defied reason. Yet, it was not the sea serpents or the violent storm that weighed most heavily on his mind—it was his navigator, Juan Niño de La Rota.

For weeks, Columbus had relied on Niño's expertise to guide the fleet through uncharted waters. The man had proven himself time and time again, navigating through storms, calming the crew during moments of panic, and guiding them through treacherous currents with an ease that bordered on the uncanny. But after the recent attack, Columbus had begun to notice things—small, subtle details that made him question just how much Niño truly knew.

As the fleet sailed westward, Niño was often found at the bow of the ship, his dark eyes fixed on the stars above or the horizon ahead, as if he could see something the others could not. He rarely spoke of his methods, and when he did, his answers were vague, often leaving more questions than answers. It was as though Niño was keeping something hidden—something deeper, more ancient than simple navigational skill.

Columbus watched as Niño stood at the bow now, his posture calm and focused, even after the chaos they had just survived. The other men were still shaken, their nerves frayed from the attack, but Niño seemed as steady as ever, almost as if he had expected the creatures.

A suspicion had begun to creep into Columbus' mind. Could it be that Niño knew more about these waters than he was letting on? There had always been rumors surrounding the man—whispers among the crew about his heritage, about his rumored connection to ancient navigators who had crossed seas long before the Europeans. And there were the tales of his African ancestry, of knowledge passed down through generations that had been lost to most of the world.

Columbus approached Niño, his boots clicking against the wooden deck as he walked. The wind had picked up again, though it was a gentle breeze, and the smell of salt filled the air. As Columbus neared, Niño turned slightly, acknowledging his presence with a nod but saying nothing. The silence between them was heavy, thick with unspoken thoughts.

"Niño," Columbus began, his voice measured, "you've guided us well through these dangerous waters. But there's something I must ask."

Niño's gaze remained fixed on the horizon. "What is it, Admiral?"

Columbus paused, choosing his words carefully. "You've demonstrated a knowledge that goes beyond what I've seen in any other navigator. You read the stars as if they are familiar to you, even in waters no European has ever sailed. And when those creatures attacked... you didn't seem surprised."

Niño's eyes flicked briefly to Columbus, his expression unreadable. "I've been on the sea for many years. I've learned to expect the unexpected."

Columbus frowned. "This is different. You've been calm in the face of dangers that no man should have known were coming. I need to know—what is it you're not telling me?"

For a long moment, Niño said nothing. The wind tugged at his cloak, and the waves gently rocked the ship beneath them. When he finally spoke, his voice was quiet but firm, as though he had made a decision to share something he had long kept hidden.

"I come from a line of navigators, Admiral," Niño said, his eyes drifting toward the stars once more. "Not just sailors, but men who studied the oceans, the stars, and the creatures that dwell within them. My ancestors sailed these waters long before Europeans ever dreamed of crossing the Atlantic. They knew the dangers that lurk in the deep, and they passed that knowledge down, generation after generation."

Columbus narrowed his eyes. "Your ancestors? You speak of African sailors?"

Niño nodded slowly. "Yes, some were from the great empires of Mali and others from the coasts further south. They knew the seas as well as the desert caravans knew the sands. They had their own maps, their own stars to guide them. And they spoke of creatures—beings that lived in the deep, in waters untouched by the hand of man."

Columbus felt a chill run down his spine. He had heard rumors of ancient African voyages, of sailors who might have crossed the seas long before the Europeans. But to hear it from Niño's own lips was something else entirely.

"These sea serpents," Niño continued, his voice calm but laced with something darker, "they have been in these waters for centuries. My people knew of them, though few dared to speak of them openly. They're not just animals. They are guardians of these waters, protectors of the deep. They don't attack unless provoked or unless they sense something... unnatural."

Columbus's brow furrowed. "Unnatural? What do you mean?"

Niño's eyes flicked to the sky, then back to Columbus. "There are forces at play here, Admiral, forces that we do not fully understand. The sea is vast, and it holds many secrets—some ancient, some dangerous. The serpents are just one part of that. We may have ventured into waters where men are not welcome."

Columbus's mouth went dry. He had always considered himself a man of science, a man of logic, but there was something in Niño's words that rang true in a way that was both unsettling and undeniable. It was as if Niño was speaking of a world beneath the world, a realm of ancient powers and creatures that operated beyond the understanding of ordinary men.

"So you knew these creatures were here," Columbus said, his voice low, almost accusing.

"I suspected," Niño replied, his tone even. "But I did not know for certain until they revealed themselves. They are watching us, Admiral. They are testing us."

Columbus was silent for a moment, grappling with the weight of Niño's words. He had always believed this voyage to be one of discovery, of charting unknown waters and claiming new lands for Spain. But now, as he stood beside Niño, staring out at the vast, dark sea, he realized that they might have ventured into something far more dangerous than he had ever imagined.

"Why didn't you warn me?" Columbus asked, a hint of frustration creeping into his voice.

Niño turned to face him fully now, his dark eyes meeting Columbus's with quiet intensity. "Would you have believed me? Would the men have believed me if I told them tales of sea monsters and ancient powers? No, Admiral. I've been guiding us as best I can, but some things cannot be explained—only survived."

Columbus's jaw clenched. He wanted to be angry, wanted to demand more answers, but deep down, he knew Niño was right. This voyage had become something else, something far beyond his control. And Niño, with his knowledge of the stars and the creatures of the deep, was their only hope of navigating through it.

"I trust you," Columbus said finally, his voice soft but resolute. "But you must trust me as well. If we are to survive this journey, I need to know everything you know."

Niño inclined his head, his expression unreadable. "Very well, Admiral. But know this—what we face is not just the wrath of the sea.

There are powers in these waters that go back farther than any of us. And if we are to survive, we must tread carefully."

Columbus nodded, though his heart was heavy with uncertainty. As he walked away from Niño and returned to the helm, he couldn't shake the feeling that they were no longer the masters of their own fate. The sea, with all its mysteries and dangers, had taken control of their destiny, and the only thing they could do now was follow its lead.

And as the fleet sailed deeper into the unknown, Columbus couldn't help but wonder—what other secrets did Niño carry, and how much more would they have to endure before they reached the end of their journey?

Part III: Descent into Desperation
Chapter 10: The Curse of the Abyss

The day had started like many others, with the sun climbing lazily into the sky and the fleet cutting through the open sea under clear skies. For a brief time, the terror of the serpents seemed a distant memory, and the crew allowed themselves a moment of cautious relief. The waters were calm, the wind steady, and the ships moved effortlessly through the vast expanse of blue. But beneath that serenity, something darker stirred.

Among the crew, there was one sailor who had been growing increasingly erratic over the past few days. His name was Mateo, a quiet, unassuming man from a small fishing village on the Spanish coast. He had signed up for the voyage with dreams of fortune and adventure, but like many of the men, the endless days at sea and the mounting dangers had begun to weigh on him. In the days since the sea serpents' attack, Mateo had become withdrawn, his eyes constantly flicking toward the horizon, as if expecting something terrible to emerge from the depths at any moment.

The first signs of his unraveling were subtle. He muttered to himself at night, talking in his sleep about things no one could understand—strange, half-formed words about the sea and creatures that lurked beneath the waves. At first, the other sailors dismissed it as the ramblings of a man shaken by the attack. But as the days wore on, Mateo's behavior became more erratic.

It was just after dawn when the crew of the *Santa Maria* began to notice something was wrong. Mateo had been assigned to the night watch, a task that required him to keep a vigilant eye on the sea while the others rested. But when the next watchman came to relieve him, they found Mateo standing at the bow of the ship, staring out at the water, his eyes wide and wild.

"Mateo?" the watchman called, stepping forward cautiously. "Are you all right?"

Mateo didn't respond at first. His gaze remained fixed on the water, his hands gripping the rail so tightly that his knuckles had turned white. The watchman took another step closer, his concern growing.

"Mateo?"

Finally, Mateo turned, and the watchman recoiled at the sight of his face. His eyes were bloodshot, dark circles ringing them as though he hadn't slept in days. His skin was pale, almost sickly, and his lips trembled as he spoke.

"They're pulling us," Mateo whispered, his voice barely audible. "They're pulling the ship... into the abyss."

The watchman blinked, confused. "What are you talking about?"

Mateo pointed out to the water, his hand trembling. "I saw them. In the night. They were out there—beneath the waves. They're pulling us toward something. A whirlpool. A dark place... where no man should go."

The watchman followed Mateo's gaze but saw nothing but the calm surface of the ocean. "Mateo, there's nothing out there. You're just tired—come on, let's get you some rest."

But Mateo shook his head violently, backing away from the rail. "No, no, you don't understand! They're out there! Mermaids! I saw them with my own eyes, their pale faces, their long hair trailing in the water. They were singing... calling to me... pulling the ship toward the abyss!"

By now, a few of the other sailors had gathered around, drawn by the commotion. They exchanged uneasy glances, unsure whether to believe Mateo's wild ravings or dismiss them as the product of exhaustion and fear. But Mateo's voice had grown louder, more frantic.

"They're leading us to our doom!" he shouted, pointing wildly at the water. "If we don't turn back, we'll all be swallowed by the whirlpool! It's there, just beyond the horizon. I can feel it!"

The men shifted uncomfortably. They had faced storms and sea monsters, but now they were confronted with something far more insidious—the fear of madness, creeping into the minds of the crew. Some of them had heard the old legends, stories of sailors driven mad by the sea, by the things they claimed to see in the water. Was this what was happening to Mateo?

Before anyone could stop him, Mateo let out a terrified scream and lunged toward the edge of the ship, as if trying to escape the invisible force he believed was pulling them into the abyss. Several of the men rushed forward, grabbing him before he could throw himself overboard, but Mateo struggled against them, his eyes wild with terror.

"They're coming for us!" he screamed, thrashing against their grip. "The mermaids! The abyss! We're doomed! We're all doomed!"

"Get him below deck!" one of the officers barked, and the men dragged Mateo, kicking and screaming, away from the rail. His cries echoed across the deck as they hauled him down into the ship's hold, his voice growing fainter but no less desperate.

As the crew stood in stunned silence, Columbus and Niño approached, both having been alerted to the commotion. Columbus's face was grim, his eyes flicking to the men who stood around, murmuring in hushed tones about what Mateo had said.

"What happened?" Columbus demanded.

One of the sailors shook his head. "It's Mateo, Admiral. He's lost his mind. He's been raving about mermaids and a whirlpool, saying they're pulling the ship into some kind of abyss."

Columbus cursed under his breath. The last thing he needed was for the crew to start believing in such madness. With every passing day, their morale had grown more fragile, and Mateo's ravings were sure to plant seeds of fear in their minds.

"Don't listen to him," Columbus said loudly, addressing the men. "He's just exhausted. The sea has gotten to him, but we're still on course. There's no whirlpool, no mermaids. We'll continue westward as planned."

But as Columbus spoke, he noticed the way the men glanced uneasily at one another. Mateo's words had struck a chord, igniting the same fear that lingered in the back of their minds—fear of the unknown, of the vast and mysterious ocean that stretched endlessly before them.

Niño, standing beside Columbus, remained silent, his eyes fixed on the water. He had seen this kind of fear before, the way the sea could unravel even the strongest of minds. But there was something about Mateo's ravings that bothered him. The sailor had mentioned a whirlpool, a dark abyss that pulled ships to their doom. It was a story Niño had heard before, from the old navigators, men who had sailed too far into uncharted waters and returned with tales of strange, magnetic forces in the ocean, whirlpools that seemed to appear out of nowhere, drawing ships into the deep.

Niño approached the rail, peering down into the water. The surface was calm, but beneath it, he could feel something—an unsettling presence, as though the sea itself was watching, waiting.

"Do you think it's possible?" Columbus asked quietly, stepping up beside him. "What Mateo said—about the mermaids, the whirlpool?"

Niño didn't answer right away. Instead, he looked out at the horizon, where the sky seemed to darken, just slightly, as if a shadow was creeping across the water.

"I don't know," Niño said finally, his voice low. "But I've heard stories. Stories of places in the ocean where strange things happen—places where the sea itself seems cursed."

Columbus frowned. "You think this is one of those places?"

Niño met his gaze, his expression unreadable. "Perhaps. Or perhaps it's just the fear talking. But we should be cautious, Admiral. The ocean holds many secrets, and not all of them are meant to be understood."

Columbus said nothing, but his mind raced. He had come on this voyage with dreams of discovery and conquest, but the further they sailed, the more he realized how little he truly knew about the world beyond the horizon. There were forces at work here—forces that defied logic, that made men see things they couldn't explain.

As the sun set and darkness fell over the sea, the men of the fleet huddled together, speaking in hushed voices about Mateo's warnings. They glanced nervously at the water, wondering if there was something down there, something waiting to pull them into the abyss.

And below deck, in the dim light of the ship's hold, Mateo lay in his hammock, his eyes wide with terror. He could still hear the voices—the voices of the mermaids, calling to him from the deep, their song pulling him toward a place where the sea swallowed all who ventured too far.

The abyss was waiting. And soon, it would claim them all.

Chapter 11: Mutiny in the Night

The tension aboard the *Santa Maria* was now palpable, a suffocating blanket that pressed down on the crew as they sailed further into the unknown. Mateo's descent into madness had shaken the men to their core. His frantic warnings of mermaids and a whirlpool haunted their thoughts, even as Columbus dismissed them as the ravings of a broken mind. But fear had a way of spreading like wildfire, and as the days passed with no sight of land, that fear began to consume the crew.

The once-disciplined sailors had grown restless, their nerves frayed from weeks of uncertainty, hunger, and exhaustion. The sea, once a source of opportunity, now seemed like a prison, with no end in sight. Every creak of the ship, every gust of wind, felt like a prelude to some new horror lurking beneath the waves.

It was in the dead of night, under a moonless sky, that the seeds of mutiny began to take root.

Below deck, in the dimly lit galley of the *Santa Maria*, a group of sailors gathered in secret. Their faces were hard and pale, their eyes flickering with fear and desperation. At the center of the group stood Vicente, a burly sailor with a reputation for speaking his mind. He had been one of the first to voice his doubts about the voyage, and now, with Mateo's warnings echoing in their heads, he had begun to speak of something even more dangerous—mutiny.

"We've had enough," Vicente hissed, his voice barely a whisper but filled with urgency. "Columbus is leading us to our deaths. Every day we sail further into the unknown, and what have we found? Monsters, storms, and madness. If we don't turn back now, none of us will live to see Spain again."

The men around him muttered in agreement, their expressions grim. They had all seen what happened to Mateo. They had felt the same terror when the sea serpents attacked. And with every passing day, their hope of reaching the Indies grew fainter, replaced by the gnawing fear that they were heading straight into the abyss.

"We should have turned back weeks ago," one of the younger sailors said, his voice trembling. "We're all going to die out here."

Vicente nodded. "That's exactly why we need to act now. We can't trust Columbus anymore. He's blinded by his ambition, and he'll lead us straight into whatever cursed waters Mateo was raving about. We need to take control of the ship and head back to Spain before it's too late."

The men exchanged uneasy glances. Mutiny was not something they had ever imagined when they signed up for this voyage, but the fear of what lay ahead was greater than their fear of disobedience. And Vicente's words were starting to make sense. If they didn't act soon, there might not be anyone left to return.

"But how do we do it?" one of the sailors asked, his brow furrowed. "Columbus is always surrounded by his officers. And what about Niño? He seems to know everything that's going on aboard the ship. He'll see us coming before we have a chance to act."

Vicente's expression darkened. "Niño is part of the problem. He's been guiding us into danger this whole time. I don't trust him any more than I trust Columbus. They're in this together. But we outnumber them. If we strike quickly, we can take control of the ship before they know what's happening."

The men murmured their agreement, though their fear was still evident. They knew that mutiny was a dangerous path, but in their minds, it had become the only option. They would overthrow Columbus, seize control of the *Santa Maria*, and chart a course back to Spain. If they succeeded, they would return as heroes for surviving the horrors of the voyage. If they failed... well, they didn't want to think about that.

As the men continued to plan, they didn't notice the figure standing in the shadows just beyond the galley's entrance. Niño had been making his usual rounds of the ship, ensuring that all was in order, when he overheard the whispers of dissent. His sharp eyes and keen instincts had led him to the galley, where he now listened quietly to the mutiny unfolding before him.

For a moment, Niño's heart sank. He had suspected that the crew's morale was weakening, but he hadn't anticipated that it had deteriorated to the point of mutiny. He knew that if these men acted on their plans, it would lead to chaos, possibly bloodshed. And if they turned the ship around, there was no guarantee they would survive the journey back to Spain. The sea was unforgiving, and turning back now might spell doom for them all.

Niño needed to act, and he needed to act quickly.

He stepped out of the shadows, his presence immediately felt by the men in the galley. The room fell silent as the sailors turned to face him, their eyes widening in surprise and fear. Vicente's hand instinctively went to the knife at his belt, but he hesitated, unsure of what Niño might do.

"I see you've been busy," Niño said calmly, his voice low but commanding. He took a step forward, his dark eyes scanning the group. "Plotting mutiny in the dead of night? Do you really think this is the answer?"

Vicente stiffened, his grip tightening on his knife. "We don't have a choice, Niño. Columbus is leading us to our deaths, and you're helping him. We can't keep sailing into these cursed waters. We need to go back before it's too late."

Niño raised an eyebrow, his expression unreadable. "And you think mutiny will save you? You think turning back now will ensure your survival?"

"We can't keep following Columbus!" Vicente shot back, his voice rising with anger. "He's blinded by his dream of reaching the Indies. We've already lost men, and it'll only get worse. If we don't act, we'll all end up dead."

Niño nodded slowly, as if considering Vicente's words. He glanced around the room, meeting the eyes of each man in turn. He could see the fear in their faces, the desperation. But he also saw something else—doubt. Doubt that mutiny would actually solve anything. Doubt that turning back would truly bring them safety.

"You're right about one thing," Niño said quietly. "This voyage has been dangerous. We've faced storms, sea monsters, and worse. But turning back now won't save us. The sea is unpredictable, and the journey back to Spain could be just as perilous as the journey forward."

The men exchanged uneasy glances, but Vicente's face remained hard. "So what are we supposed to do, then? Just follow Columbus blindly until we're all dead?"

Niño shook his head. "No. But you need to understand something—Columbus may be ambitious, but he's not a fool. He knows the risks, just as I do. And if you think I'm blindly following him, you're mistaken. I've been guiding this ship because I believe that we can make it to the other side. But it won't happen if we tear ourselves apart from within."

The room was silent again, the weight of Niño's words settling over the men like a heavy fog.

"We're closer than you think," Niño continued, his voice calm but firm. "The sea is testing us, yes. But we've survived this long because we've worked together. If we start fighting among ourselves, we'll be lost—no matter which direction we sail."

Vicente's eyes flickered with uncertainty, his grip on the knife loosening slightly. "And if you're wrong? If we keep going and there's nothing out there but more death?"

Niño took a step closer, his gaze steady. "Then we'll face it together. But if you act on this mutiny now, you'll be condemning us all. I can't force you to trust me, but I can promise you this—we will not survive if we turn on each other."

For a long, tense moment, the men said nothing. Vicente stood frozen, his jaw clenched, his hand still hovering near his knife. But Niño's words had struck a chord, and the fire of rebellion that had been burning in his eyes seemed to flicker, dimming just slightly.

Finally, Vicente let out a slow breath and stepped back, releasing his grip on the knife. "What do we do, then?"

Niño allowed a small, relieved smile to tug at the corner of his mouth. "We keep sailing. We trust in the sea, and in each other. And when the time comes, we'll make our move. But not like this."

The men, still shaken but calmer now, nodded in agreement. The threat of mutiny had been diffused, for the moment, but Niño knew that the seeds of fear had been planted deeply. He would have to keep a close eye on Vicente and the others in the days to come. Trust was a fragile thing out here on the open sea.

As the men dispersed and returned to their duties, Niño lingered in the galley for a moment, his thoughts racing. He had stopped the mutiny for now, but he knew that the journey ahead would only grow more dangerous. The sea had its secrets, and they were sailing straight into the heart of them.

Columbus was still at the helm, unaware of how close he had come to losing control of his ship. And as Niño made his way back to the deck, he couldn't help but wonder—how much longer could he keep the crew from tearing themselves apart, and what other dangers awaited them in the dark waters ahead?

Chapter 12: The Ghost Ship

The air was thick with the scent of salt and the quiet hum of the wind as the fleet sailed deeper into uncharted waters. After the tension of the previous nights, a wary calm had settled over the *Santa Maria*, *Pinta*, and *Niña*. The sailors kept their heads down, tending to their duties in silence, haunted by the near-mutiny and the dangers they had already faced. Even Niño, ever watchful, sensed that the ocean was holding its breath, as if waiting for something.

It came in the stillness of the afternoon.

The lookout atop the *Santa Maria*'s mast was the first to spot it—a dark shape on the horizon, drifting aimlessly in the water. At first, it was thought to be a small island or perhaps a large mass of seaweed, but as they drew closer, it became clear that it was something far more unsettling.

"Ship ahead!" the lookout shouted, his voice echoing across the deck. "To the starboard side!"

Columbus immediately snapped to attention, his heart racing at the prospect of encountering another vessel in these remote waters. Could it be another explorer? A lost merchant ship blown off course by the same storms they had survived? He quickly ordered the fleet to adjust course and intercept the ship.

As the *Santa Maria* and her companions approached the mysterious vessel, the details became clearer. It was an old ship, its hull weathered and darkened by the sea. The sails hung limp, tattered and torn, as though they had not been used in years. The ship drifted aimlessly on the water, carried only by the current, with no sign of life aboard. The closer they got, the more uneasy the crew became.

"There's no one aboard," one of the sailors muttered under his breath, his face pale. "It's a ghost ship."

Niño, standing near the helm, narrowed his eyes as he studied the ship. It was an eerie sight—too quiet, too still. Something about it felt wrong, like it didn't belong in this world. He couldn't shake the feeling that they were about to uncover something dangerous, something they weren't meant to see.

As the *Santa Maria* pulled alongside the drifting ship, Columbus ordered a small party of men to board it and investigate. Vicente, one of the sailors who had been involved in the near-mutiny, volunteered to lead the group. He was eager to prove himself after the events of the previous night, and perhaps to banish the fear that still gnawed at his heart.

Niño watched as Vicente and the others climbed aboard the ghostly vessel. From the *Santa Maria*, the rest of the crew could only see the men moving slowly across the deck, their figures small and shadowy against the backdrop of the abandoned ship. The silence that followed was deafening, broken only by the gentle creaking of the ships as they swayed in the current.

Minutes passed, and then Vicente's voice rang out from the deck of the ghost ship.

"There's no one here!" he called, though there was an edge of unease in his tone. "No sign of a crew. It looks like it's been abandoned for a long time."

Columbus frowned, exchanging a glance with Niño. Abandoned ships were not uncommon in the dangerous waters of the open sea, but something about this vessel didn't sit right with either of them. There should have been signs of struggle—damage from a storm, perhaps, or remnants of the crew's belongings. But from what they could see, the ship was strangely intact, as if it had been left to drift on the ocean by something far more sinister.

Niño gestured to one of the other men on the *Santa Maria*. "We need to take a closer look."

Columbus nodded, and Niño quickly made his way onto the small boat that would ferry him to the ghost ship. As they crossed the short distance between the two vessels, Niño's thoughts churned. The sea had shown them many strange things, but this... this felt different. It felt wrong.

When Niño climbed aboard the ghost ship, the first thing he noticed was the smell—a faint, musty odor, like damp wood and something else... something old and decaying. The ship's deck was covered in a thin layer of grime, but there were no signs of rot or significant damage. The masts stood tall, though the sails were shredded, flapping limply in the wind.

But it was the silence that unnerved him the most. The ship was utterly still, as though it had been frozen in time.

Vicente approached him, his face pale and drawn. "There's something you should see," he said, his voice low. "In the captain's quarters."

Niño followed Vicente through the eerie silence of the ship's interior, the wooden floorboards creaking beneath their feet. As they approached the door to the captain's quarters, Niño felt a chill run down his spine. The air here was colder, as though something had taken the warmth from the ship and left behind only the chill of death.

Vicente pushed open the door, revealing a dimly lit cabin. The room was sparse, with a small desk and a few pieces of broken furniture. But what caught Niño's attention were the walls. Strange symbols, unlike anything he had ever seen, were carved into the wood. They spiraled and twisted in patterns that made no sense, like the markings of some long-forgotten language.

Niño approached the carvings, running his fingers lightly over the rough surface. The symbols were deep, as though someone had painstakingly etched them into the hull. But they weren't just random shapes. There was an intelligence behind them, a purpose. They seemed to radiate a sense of doom, as if they were a warning to anyone who dared to enter this ship.

"What do you think it means?" Vicente asked, his voice trembling slightly.

Niño shook his head. "I don't know. But whatever it is, it's not good."

As Niño studied the symbols, he noticed something else—a small, weathered book lying on the desk, half-buried under a pile of dust. He reached for it, carefully brushing away the dirt, revealing the worn leather cover. The book looked ancient, its pages yellowed and fragile.

Niño opened it slowly, his eyes scanning the strange, indecipherable text inside. The writing was similar to the symbols on the walls, though more structured, as if it were part of a larger script. He couldn't read it, but the more he looked at it, the more a sense of dread filled him.

"This ship..." Vicente muttered, his voice barely a whisper. "It feels cursed."

Niño nodded in agreement, his eyes still fixed on the pages of the book. "Whatever happened here, it wasn't natural."

Just as Niño closed the book, a sudden gust of wind howled through the ship, slamming the door to the captain's quarters shut with a loud bang. Both men jumped, their hearts racing. The wind had picked up, swirling around the ship like an unseen force, stirring the air with a cold, unnatural intensity.

"We need to leave," Vicente said quickly, his eyes wide with fear. "Now."

Niño didn't argue. There was something dark and ancient about this ship, something that had no place in the world of men. He tucked the strange book under his arm and hurried out of the cabin, Vicente close behind. As they made their way back to the deck, the wind continued to howl, and the eerie silence that had once filled the ship was replaced by an overwhelming sense of foreboding.

When Niño and Vicente finally returned to the *Santa Maria*, the crew gathered around them, their faces pale and anxious. Columbus stepped forward, his eyes narrowing as he saw the fear in their expressions.

"What did you find?" Columbus asked.

Niño handed him the book, his voice low. "Something... ancient. And these symbols—they're carved into the walls of the ship. I don't know what they mean, but I fear it's a warning."

Columbus frowned, flipping through the pages of the book. "A warning of what?"

Niño looked back at the ghost ship, its dark silhouette looming in the distance. "I don't know. But whatever happened to that crew... it wasn't natural."

The men stood in uneasy silence, their eyes drifting to the abandoned vessel that now seemed to float like a specter on the water. The strange symbols carved into its hull, the book filled with unreadable text—everything about the ship felt like a dark omen.

And as night began to fall over the sea, casting long shadows across the water, the crew could not shake the feeling that they had stumbled upon something far more dangerous than they could comprehend.

The ghost ship drifted behind them, but its presence lingered, haunting their thoughts. And the strange symbols, foretelling doom, seemed to mark the beginning of a new terror on their cursed voyage into the unknown.

Chapter 13: Dark Skies

The days following the discovery of the ghost ship were unsettling, to say the least. The eerie vessel had been left behind, fading into the horizon, but its ominous presence lingered in the minds of the crew. It wasn't just the strange symbols carved into the hull or the mysterious book Niño had recovered—it was the way the ship seemed to carry a dark energy with it, as though it had left an imprint on the sea itself.

As the fleet sailed onward, the weather began to change. The sun, which had been their constant companion on the journey westward, disappeared behind a thick layer of clouds. At first, it seemed like an ordinary shift in the weather, a temporary overcast sky that would pass in a day or two. But as the days stretched on, the clouds only grew heavier, darker, smothering the horizon in a grim, oppressive gray.

The sea became a dull, featureless expanse, with no sun to light their way and no stars to guide them by night. The winds, too, seemed to grow weaker, leaving the ships to drift slowly through the water, their sails barely stirring. The air itself felt heavy, thick with moisture, as though a storm was brewing just beyond sight. But the storm never came. Instead, the sky remained dark, an unrelenting shroud that hung over the fleet like a curse.

Niño stood at the helm of the *Santa Maria*, his eyes scanning the sky for any break in the clouds. It had been days since he had last seen the stars, and without them, navigation had become nearly impossible. The maps were useless now—without the stars to guide them, they were sailing blind. Even the compass seemed to have lost its reliability, the needle flickering uncertainly as if confused by some unseen force.

The crew, already shaken by the events of the past weeks, had grown more anxious with each passing day. The ghost ship, the sea serpents, Mateo's madness—it all seemed to be building toward something, some dark culmination that they could neither predict nor understand.

And now, with the sky permanently overcast, a new sense of dread began to settle over the men.

Niño had always been the calm one, the steady presence in the face of danger. But even he felt the weight of uncertainty pressing down on him. He had never encountered weather like this, a sky that refused to clear, a sea that seemed to be holding its breath. The other men looked to him for guidance, but for the first time, he wasn't sure what to tell them. Without the stars, he felt lost.

Columbus approached him one evening, his expression tight with concern. The sky above them was a flat, dark gray, the clouds thick enough to blot out the sun completely. It was as if night had fallen early, the world bathed in a strange, dim twilight that never seemed to end.

"Have you seen anything?" Columbus asked, his voice low, as though speaking too loudly would somehow upset the delicate balance of the sea and sky.

Niño shook his head, his gaze fixed on the horizon. "Nothing. No stars, no landmarks. We're drifting, Admiral. And without the stars, there's no way to be certain of our course."

Columbus clenched his jaw, glancing up at the darkened sky. "We can't keep going like this. The men are growing restless."

Niño didn't need to be told. He could feel the crew's unease growing with each passing day. They whispered to one another in hushed tones, casting nervous glances at the sky, as if expecting some terrible force to emerge from the clouds at any moment. They spoke of curses, of ancient evils they had awakened by venturing too far into unknown waters. And though Niño didn't believe in such things, the unbroken darkness above them made it hard to dismiss the fear entirely.

"I know," Niño said quietly. "But there's nothing we can do. Until the sky clears, we're at the mercy of the sea."

Columbus sighed, running a hand through his hair. "How much longer can we last like this? The supplies are running low, and the men are starting to talk about turning back."

Niño turned to look at him, his expression grim. "And what would we turn back to? We're in uncharted waters. Without the stars, we could be sailing in circles. Turning back might take us nowhere."

Columbus fell silent, staring out at the vast, empty sea. He had led the fleet with confidence and ambition, driven by the promise of discovery and glory. But now, that confidence was slipping. The ocean felt different now, more like a trap than a pathway to the Indies. And for the first time since the voyage began, Columbus wasn't sure he had the strength to keep pushing forward.

The days blurred together, one after the other, the sky remaining stubbornly overcast. The crew's nerves were fraying, their tempers short. Men who had once been eager for adventure now muttered darkly about the cursed voyage, about how they had been led to their doom by Columbus' ambition. Some spoke openly of turning back, while others whispered of the ghost ship, claiming that it had marked them with its symbols, cursed them to sail forever under a dark sky.

Niño felt the weight of their fear pressing down on him, but more than that, he felt his own doubts creeping in. He had always trusted the sea, always relied on the stars to guide him. But now, with the sky refusing to show its face, he felt lost in a way he had never experienced before. He had been the one who kept the men steady, who kept Columbus from losing his resolve. But now, even Niño wasn't sure how much longer he could keep going.

One night, after the sun had set—though there was little difference between night and day now—Niño stood alone on the deck, staring up at the sky. The clouds were thick and dark, the moon completely hidden behind their oppressive weight. The air was still, almost suffocating, and the silence was broken only by the gentle lapping of the waves against the ship's hull.

For the first time in weeks, Niño felt a pang of fear deep in his chest. What if they were lost? What if the voyage had been doomed from the start, and they were now drifting toward some unseen abyss?

The strange symbols on the ghost ship, Mateo's ravings about the abyss—were they all warnings of some terrible fate that awaited them?

Niño's hands tightened on the rail as he gazed out into the darkness. He had always trusted the sea, always believed that the ocean would guide him if he knew how to listen. But now, for the first time, he wasn't sure if the sea was on their side anymore. It felt as though they had ventured too far, crossed a line they were never meant to cross.

He closed his eyes, trying to push the thoughts away, but the silence was too loud, the darkness too deep.

The next morning, the crew awoke to find the sky unchanged—still dark, still ominous. The men moved about their duties with grim determination, but the spark of hope that had once driven them had faded. They were drifting, lost in a sea that no longer seemed to offer them any way forward.

As the days wore on, even Columbus began to lose faith. He stood at the helm, staring out at the endless horizon with empty eyes, his once-bold vision of discovery clouded by doubt. The men no longer looked to him for guidance. They worked in silence, their faces gaunt and pale, their eyes hollow with fear.

And still, the sky remained dark.

Niño stood at the bow, his heart heavy with uncertainty. He had always been the one to lead them through the darkness, but now even he could feel the weight of doubt pressing down on him. He didn't know what lay ahead, didn't know if they would ever see the stars again. All he knew was that the sky had turned against them, and the sea was no longer a friend.

The dark skies stretched on, unbroken, and with each passing day, hope slipped further from their grasp.

They were lost.

Chapter 14: The Siren's Song

The nights had grown colder, darker, and more oppressive. The sky, still thick with unbroken clouds, offered no relief from the deep gloom that hung over the fleet. The days were long stretches of silence and fear, but it was the nights that truly unsettled the crew. The endless twilight seemed to suffocate any hope of finding their way, and the sea, once full of life, had become a vast, empty void. Each night, the sense of isolation grew heavier, as if the ocean was slowly swallowing them.

But then, the silence of the night was broken by something far worse.

It started as a soft sound, barely audible above the creaking of the ship and the lapping of the waves. A melody, delicate and haunting, that seemed to rise from the depths of the ocean itself. The first to hear it were the men on the night watch. They leaned over the rails, peering into the darkness, unsure of what they were hearing.

"I thought I heard something," one of the younger sailors muttered to his companion, his voice uneasy. "Like singing."

His companion scoffed, though there was fear in his eyes. "You've been at sea too long, boy. There's no singing out here."

But the melody persisted, growing more distinct as the night wore on. It was a strange, otherworldly tune—beautiful, yet filled with a sense of sorrow, like a lament carried on the wind. The longer the sailors listened, the more they felt its pull, a deep, instinctual yearning that tugged at their hearts. It called to them, beckoning them to the water, to the dark, cold sea just beyond the edge of the ship.

By the time the rest of the crew woke the next morning, rumors had already spread. The men on the night watch claimed to have heard voices—singing from the sea, soft and sweet, like a lullaby meant to soothe them. Some dismissed it as the ramblings of tired minds, but others felt the same uneasy pull, the same nagging sense that something out there was calling to them.

Columbus, however, was having none of it. He stormed across the deck, his frustration evident as he barked orders. "Enough with these foolish stories! You're sailors, not children frightened by ghost tales. There's nothing out there but the sea, and we'll keep moving until we find land!"

But his words did little to calm the growing fear among the crew. Even Niño, who had always been the most rational among them, found himself unsettled by the whispers of the men. Something about the way they described the music felt too real to dismiss as simple superstition. The sea had shown them many strange and dangerous things, and Niño had learned not to take any sign from the ocean lightly.

That night, the singing returned.

This time, more men heard it. The eerie melody drifted over the water, soft but insistent, weaving through the ship like a spectral presence. The sound was impossible to ignore. It seemed to seep into their minds, filling them with a sense of longing, a desperate need to follow the sound to its source.

Niño stood on the deck, listening. He felt the music, too—an almost magnetic pull that made his heart race, as if it were speaking directly to him. But he forced himself to remain still, his hands gripping the ship's rail tightly as he fought against the strange urge to follow the song. He could see the effect it was having on the others, their eyes wide and distant, their bodies swaying slightly as though they were entranced.

Suddenly, a shout rang out from the far side of the ship.

One of the sailors, a man named Pedro, had leapt over the rail and plunged into the water below. The men rushed to the side, shouting his name, but Pedro didn't respond. His body disappeared into the dark waves, the sound of the haunting melody lingering in the air as if it had pulled him down into the depths.

"Man overboard!" someone yelled, but it was already too late. Pedro was gone.

Panic rippled through the crew as they desperately searched the water, but there was no sign of Pedro. He had vanished beneath the waves, lost to the sea, and the song continued, as if taunting them with its power.

"What is happening?" one of the sailors cried, his voice trembling. "Why did he jump?"

"He heard the music," another replied, his face pale. "He heard it and... and it made him go. It's the sirens!"

The word "sirens" passed through the crew like a curse. They had all heard the stories—creatures of legend who lured sailors to their doom with their enchanting voices. Many had dismissed such tales as mere superstition, but now, with Pedro gone and the strange, haunting melody echoing through the night, the men began to wonder if the old stories were true after all.

"We need to stop the ship," one of the officers said urgently to Columbus. "If this is what we think it is, we can't keep going. The men are terrified."

Columbus, clearly shaken by the loss of Pedro, hesitated. He didn't want to believe in the sirens, in these ancient legends that defied reason. But the fear in the men's eyes was undeniable, and the strange, magnetic pull of the song was something he could not explain.

"We press on," he said, though his voice lacked its usual certainty. "We stay vigilant. No one else goes overboard. We tie the men down if we have to."

But as the night wore on, the song grew louder, more insistent. It wove through the ship like a living thing, wrapping itself around the minds of the crew, pulling at their thoughts, their hearts. One by one, the men began to feel its pull. Some resisted, gripping the rail or holding on to their companions, but others could not fight the temptation. They moved as if in a trance, their eyes vacant, their steps slow and deliberate.

Niño, standing at the helm, watched in horror as two more sailors broke free from the others and threw themselves overboard, their bodies disappearing into the dark water without a sound. The men screamed after them, but it was no use. The ocean swallowed them whole, leaving only the echo of the song behind.

Niño's heart pounded in his chest as he gripped the wheel tightly, his mind racing. The music was getting stronger, more irresistible. He could feel it creeping into his own thoughts, planting images of the sea in his mind, of a dark, welcoming place beneath the waves where the music would finally stop and peace would be found.

"Niño!" a voice shouted, breaking through the trance.

He turned to see Columbus rushing toward him, his face pale and drawn. "What's happening? Why are they going overboard?"

Niño shook his head, trying to clear the fog from his mind. "It's the song. It's like nothing I've ever heard before. It's drawing them in."

"We need to do something," Columbus said, his voice desperate. "We can't lose any more men."

Niño nodded, his jaw clenched. He knew that if they didn't act soon, the entire crew might succumb to the song's pull. But how could they fight something so intangible, so seductive? The sirens—if that's what they were—were no ordinary threat. They were ancient, powerful, and beyond the understanding of mortal men.

He glanced at the crew, many of whom were now tied down to prevent them from following the others into the sea. Their eyes were wide with terror, but the song still filled the air, pressing against their minds like a relentless tide.

"We anchor the ship," Niño said suddenly, his voice firm. "We stop moving. Maybe if we stay still, the song will pass."

Columbus hesitated but nodded. "Do it. We can't afford to lose anyone else."

With quick orders, the men anchored the ship, and the sails were furled. The ships came to a halt, floating aimlessly in the dark water, as the haunting melody continued to drift across the waves. The crew huddled together, their hands over their ears, desperately trying to block out the sound that seemed to crawl into their very souls.

The night stretched on, long and filled with dread. The song never stopped, but for the moment, no more men were lost. They were trapped in the siren's grasp, but at least, for now, they were still alive.

As the darkness deepened, Niño stood at the rail, his eyes scanning the black water below. The song filled his ears, pulling at him with a seductive promise of peace and escape. But he held firm, his mind focused on the task at hand. He would not let the sea take him, not yet.

But as the night wore on and the song continued, Niño couldn't shake the feeling that they were only delaying the inevitable. The sirens were out there, watching, waiting. And sooner or later, they would come for them all.

And when they did, there would be no escape.

Part IV: Monsters of the Deep
Chapter 15: The Leviathan Emerges

The morning after the haunting song had filled the night, the crew awoke in a state of exhausted relief. Though many had heard the sirens' calls and several sailors had disappeared into the black waters, the night had passed without further loss. The ships remained anchored in place, still adrift under the dark, oppressive skies that had plagued them for weeks. The men went about their duties with hollow eyes and drawn faces, haunted by the sounds of the night before.

But there was an uneasy calm hanging over the fleet, a sense that the worst was yet to come.

Niño, who had barely slept, stood at the helm of the *Santa Maria*, his eyes scanning the horizon. The sea was too still—unnervingly so. The sky, still heavy with dark clouds, cast an eerie twilight over the waters, and the wind had died down to a faint whisper, barely enough to stir the sails. Everything about the scene felt wrong, as though the sea itself was waiting for something, holding its breath in anticipation.

Columbus approached Niño, his face gaunt and weary. The events of the past few days had taken their toll on him, and the strain of keeping the crew together was evident in the deep lines around his eyes.

"Any sign of the sky clearing?" Columbus asked, though his tone suggested he wasn't hopeful.

Niño shook his head. "No. It's as if the sky has sealed us in. There's something unnatural about it, as if we've sailed into a place where the sun and stars no longer exist."

Columbus frowned, his gaze turning to the horizon. "We can't stay anchored forever. We have to keep moving."

Before Niño could respond, a sudden sound split the air—a low, rumbling noise that seemed to rise from the depths of the ocean itself. It wasn't the wail of the sirens, but something far deeper, more primal.

The sound reverberated through the hull of the ship, sending a shiver through the crew. Every man froze, their eyes wide with fear as they looked to one another, uncertain of what they had just heard.

"What was that?" one of the sailors whispered, his voice trembling.

The rumbling grew louder, a deep, unsettling vibration that seemed to come from beneath the water. Niño's heart began to race as he leaned over the side of the ship, peering into the dark waters below. For a moment, there was nothing—just the stillness of the ocean, calm and unbroken.

And then he saw it.

A shadow, vast and unfathomably large, moving just beneath the surface of the water. At first, it was difficult to make out, its form obscured by the dark depths, but as it rose closer to the surface, its sheer size became horrifyingly clear. It was a creature, far larger than any whale or sea serpent they had ever encountered, its body stretching out beneath the waves like a living mountain.

The men on deck gasped, stumbling back from the rail as the shadow continued to rise. The water around the ship began to churn, disturbed by the creature's ascent, and the low rumble grew into a deafening roar as the sea itself seemed to boil.

Niño's eyes widened in disbelief. He had heard stories of the Leviathan—a mythical sea monster said to dwell in the deepest parts of the ocean, a creature of such immense size and power that it could swallow ships whole. But he had never believed it was real. Until now.

"Leviathan..." someone whispered, their voice barely audible over the roar of the water.

And then, with a sudden, violent surge, the creature broke the surface.

The Leviathan rose from the depths like a nightmare brought to life. Its massive body, covered in thick, dark scales that shimmered in the dim light, towered over the ships, its head alone the size of the *Santa Maria*. Its eyes, glowing a sickly yellow, stared down at the fleet with an intelligence that sent a chill through the men's bones. Its long, serpentine neck undulated as it lifted its head high into the air, and when it opened its enormous jaws, rows of razor-sharp teeth gleamed in the darkness.

The crew of the *Santa Maria* stood frozen in terror, their minds unable to fully comprehend the sheer scale of the beast. The creature let out another deafening roar, shaking the very air around them. The sound was so powerful that it rattled the ships, causing the masts to creak and the rigging to whip about violently.

"Get the cannons ready!" Columbus shouted, his voice barely cutting through the chaos. "Prepare for attack!"

The men scrambled into action, but their movements were sluggish, weighed down by fear. Some of the sailors, still reeling from the effects of the sirens' song, could barely hold their weapons, their hands shaking uncontrollably. Others stood paralyzed, their eyes locked on the Leviathan as it loomed above them like a force of nature, unstoppable and merciless.

The creature's massive tail, thick and muscular, lashed out with terrifying speed, slamming into the side of the *Niña*. The ship rocked violently, wood splintering and cracking under the force of the blow. The men on deck were thrown to the ground as the ship tilted dangerously, nearly capsizing under the impact.

"Man the cannons!" Columbus yelled again, trying to rally the men as the Leviathan turned its attention to the *Santa Maria*.

Niño, his heart pounding in his chest, rushed to the ship's wheel, gripping it tightly as the massive beast moved closer. The water around the Leviathan churned violently, creating waves that slammed against the hull of the ship. Niño knew that if the creature struck the *Santa Maria* with the same force it had used on the *Niña*, they would not survive.

"We have to move!" Niño shouted to Columbus. "If we stay anchored, we're dead!"

Columbus hesitated for only a moment before nodding. "Cut the anchor! We need to get away from it!"

The men rushed to obey, frantically cutting the ropes that held the ship in place. As the anchor dropped into the sea, the *Santa Maria* lurched forward, carried by the faint wind that had returned. But the Leviathan was not so easily evaded. It let out another roar, its massive tail whipping through the water as it pursued the fleeing ship.

The cannons fired, the sound of gunfire echoing across the sea as the cannonballs struck the creature's thick scales. But the Leviathan seemed unfazed by the attack, its dark, impenetrable hide deflecting the cannon fire as though it were nothing more than pebbles.

The creature surged forward, its massive jaws opening wide as it snapped at the stern of the *Santa Maria*. The ship rocked violently, the wood groaning under the strain as the Leviathan's teeth sank into the hull. Splinters flew through the air as the beast tore a chunk of wood from the ship, water rushing in through the gaping hole left behind.

"Get to the pumps!" Columbus ordered, his voice hoarse with desperation. "We're taking on water!"

As the men rushed to control the flooding, Niño fought to steer the ship away from the creature. The Leviathan was relentless, its glowing eyes fixed on the *Santa Maria* as it continued its pursuit. The men fired another round of cannonballs, but it was no use. The creature's size and strength were far beyond anything they could have prepared for.

Just as it seemed the Leviathan would tear the ship apart, a sudden gust of wind filled the sails. The *Santa Maria* surged forward, propelled by the unexpected breeze, putting a small but precious distance between them and the beast.

Niño seized the opportunity, steering the ship in a wide arc away from the Leviathan. The creature roared in frustration, its massive tail thrashing against the water, sending waves crashing over the deck. But the wind held, carrying the *Santa Maria* further from the monster's reach.

The Leviathan, still snarling and snapping, began to sink back beneath the waves, its glowing eyes the last thing to disappear beneath the surface. The sea calmed, the waves subsiding as the creature vanished into the deep.

For a moment, no one spoke. The men stood in stunned silence, their hearts racing, their minds struggling to process what they had just survived.

"We need to repair the ship," Columbus said, his voice shaking but steady. "And pray that thing doesn't come back."

Niño nodded, though his eyes remained fixed on the water where the Leviathan had disappeared. He had seen many strange and terrifying things on this voyage, but nothing like the creature that had just attacked them. It was a reminder—a brutal reminder—that the sea held powers far greater than any man could hope to understand.

As the men worked to repair the ship, Niño glanced up at the sky, still dark and heavy with clouds. The Leviathan had emerged from the depths like a nightmare brought to life. And though it had retreated for now, Niño couldn't shake the feeling that it wasn't finished with them yet.

The sea had shown them its teeth, and Niño knew that the worst was still to come.

Chapter 16: Battling the Beast

The *Santa Maria* rocked violently as the sea churned beneath it, the Leviathan's massive form swirling beneath the waves like a shadow of doom. The brief respite provided by the wind had given the men a few moments to regroup, but it hadn't lasted long. The Leviathan had returned, its monstrous body breaking the surface of the water again with a terrifying roar, and now it seemed more determined than ever to destroy the fleet.

The cannons fired again, their thunderous booms echoing across the ocean as cannonballs sailed through the air. But, just as before, they struck the creature's thick, impenetrable scales and bounced off uselessly, splashing into the water below. The men cursed and reloaded, but their desperation was growing with each failed shot.

"Fire again!" Columbus bellowed, gripping the railing of the *Santa Maria* as the Leviathan circled their ship like a predator toying with its prey. The men obeyed, but it was clear that the cannons alone wouldn't be enough to fend off the beast.

Niño, standing beside Columbus, gritted his teeth as he watched the creature's massive form undulate through the water. Its glowing eyes burned with an eerie intelligence, and its body seemed to stretch endlessly, wrapping around the ships like a serpent tightening its coils. It was clear now that this wasn't a creature they could simply outrun. They had to fight.

But how?

"Admiral," Niño said, turning to Columbus, his voice low and urgent. "The cannons won't break through that hide. We need to focus on its weak points—its eyes, its mouth. That's the only chance we have."

Columbus nodded, though his face was grim. "How do we get close enough?"

Before Niño could respond, the Leviathan lashed out again. Its massive tail rose from the water like a dark wave and slammed into the side of the *Pinta*, sending men sprawling across the deck as the ship lurched dangerously to one side. Wood splintered and cracked, and the air was filled with the sounds of shouts and the groaning of the ship's timbers as it fought to stay afloat.

"The *Pinta* won't last much longer!" one of the officers shouted, his face pale with fear.

Niño's mind raced. They couldn't keep up this desperate struggle for long. The Leviathan was too strong, too relentless. But they had no choice—they had to fight. He glanced at the ship's rigging, then at the cannons, an idea forming in his mind.

"We need to get a cannon as close to the creature's head as possible," Niño said, his voice firm. "If we can land a shot inside its mouth, we might be able to do some real damage. But someone will need to get close enough to lure it in."

Columbus hesitated for only a second before nodding. "Then we'll bait it. Prepare a cannon on a smaller boat. We'll use the sails to distract it, and when it opens its mouth, we fire."

The crew moved into action, scrambling to lower one of the smaller lifeboats into the water. The men worked with frantic speed, rigging one of the smaller cannons onto the boat and preparing the ropes to guide it as close to the Leviathan as possible. It was a risky plan, but it was the only chance they had.

Niño stepped forward, ready to volunteer for the dangerous task, but Columbus grabbed his arm.

"I'll go," Columbus said, his voice steady despite the chaos around them. "You stay here and keep the ship moving. We can't let it pin us down."

For a moment, Niño hesitated, but then he nodded. Columbus' eyes were filled with the same resolve that had driven him to lead the voyage into these unknown waters. He wasn't just a captain now—he was a man willing to face the Leviathan himself, a leader ready to risk everything for his crew.

Columbus climbed into the boat with two of his most trusted men, and they began rowing toward the Leviathan, the small craft rocking violently in the rough waters. The men aboard the *Santa Maria* watched in tense silence as the boat drew closer to the creature. The Leviathan's massive body twisted beneath the surface, its head rising higher above the water, its glowing eyes locked on the tiny boat that dared to approach it.

Niño stood at the helm of the *Santa Maria*, his heart pounding in his chest. He knew that this was their moment of truth. If they failed, the Leviathan would destroy them all. He gave the signal, and the men aboard the *Santa Maria* unfurled one of the larger sails, waving it high in the air to distract the beast.

The Leviathan's attention flickered toward the sail for a moment, its massive jaws opening wide as it roared, sending waves crashing against the ship. The distraction had worked. The creature turned its head toward the *Santa Maria*, giving Columbus and his men the opportunity they needed.

"Now!" Niño shouted, his voice cutting through the noise of the battle.

Columbus' boat surged forward, the cannon ready. With the Leviathan's mouth wide open, Columbus gave the order to fire. The cannon shot rang out, the explosive force rocking the small boat as the cannonball sailed through the air and straight into the Leviathan's gaping maw.

For a moment, there was silence.

Then, the Leviathan let out an earth-shattering roar, its massive body convulsing violently as the cannonball exploded inside its mouth. The creature thrashed in the water, sending waves crashing over the boats and the decks of the ships. Its long, serpentine body writhed in agony, its massive tail whipping through the water with terrifying speed.

"Pull back!" Niño shouted, watching as the Leviathan's thrashing grew more erratic. "Everyone, get back!"

The men scrambled to retreat as the Leviathan reared up once more, its glowing eyes now filled with rage and pain. Blood poured from its mouth, the thick, dark liquid staining the water around it as the creature struggled to regain control.

But the cannon shot had done its damage. The Leviathan, wounded and furious, began to sink back into the depths, its enormous body dragging against the hull of the *Santa Maria* one last time. The ship groaned under the weight of the creature's massive bulk, but it held, the men bracing themselves as the Leviathan finally disappeared beneath the surface.

The sea went still.

For a long moment, the men stood in stunned silence, their hearts still racing from the battle. The water around them was dark with the creature's blood, the only sign that the Leviathan had ever existed.

Niño exhaled a shaky breath, his hands still gripping the wheel. The Leviathan was gone—wounded, perhaps, but not dead. It had retreated into the depths, and for now, they were safe.

Columbus' boat returned to the *Santa Maria*, the men aboard pale and exhausted, but alive. Columbus climbed back onto the ship, his face drawn but triumphant.

"We wounded it," he said, his voice hoarse. "But we need to keep moving before it returns."

Niño nodded, though his mind was still racing. The Leviathan had retreated, but he knew it wasn't finished with them yet. They had merely bought themselves time.

As the crew worked to repair the damage to the ships, Niño glanced out at the horizon, where the sky remained dark and heavy with clouds. The Leviathan had shown them just how powerful the ocean could be, and he knew that their journey was far from over.

The sea held many dangers, and this was only the beginning.

The beast had emerged from the depths—and it would come again.

Chapter 17: The Navigator's Past

The crew had barely begun to catch their breath after the desperate battle with the Leviathan when Niño stood at the helm, his mind racing with a thousand thoughts. The sea was calm once again, but the dark clouds still clung to the sky, heavy with an ominous presence. He had felt this danger coming long before the Leviathan rose from the depths. The signs had been there in the unnatural stillness of the sea, the whispers of the crew, and the endless dark sky that seemed to close in on them.

But now, after the battle, Niño knew they couldn't rely on luck or brute force any longer. There was more to these waters than the crew—or even Columbus—could understand. And it was time to reveal the secret he had kept close for so long.

That evening, Niño found Columbus in his quarters, poring over the ship's charts with furrowed brows. The flickering light of a lantern cast shadows on his weary face, but his determination was still clear. He glanced up as Niño entered, motioning for him to sit.

"The men are shaken," Columbus said, his voice low. "They fought well, but this... this is beyond what any of us imagined. We need answers, Niño."

Niño nodded, his eyes thoughtful as he leaned forward. "Admiral, there's something I haven't told you. Something that might explain the dangers we've been facing."

Columbus's eyes narrowed slightly, curiosity and suspicion flickering across his face. "Go on."

Niño took a deep breath, then reached into the folds of his cloak. From a small, hidden pocket, he pulled out a weathered piece of parchment. It was old—older than any chart Columbus had seen—and the edges were worn and frayed, as though it had passed through many hands over the centuries. The parchment was covered in strange, intricate symbols, and at the center of it all was a route, winding through dangerous-looking waters marked with ominous signs.

"This," Niño said, carefully unfolding the map and laying it on the table, "has been passed down through my family for generations. It's an ancient chart, older than anything you'll find in Spain's archives. My ancestors were navigators, explorers of the unknown seas. They sailed these waters long before European ships ever ventured this far."

Columbus's gaze flickered over the map, his interest piqued. "This is no ordinary map."

"No, it's not," Niño replied. "This chart shows a route through the most dangerous waters known to my ancestors. Waters that are said to be ruled by the old gods of the sea—beings far older than any civilization we know. Creatures like the Leviathan... and worse."

Columbus looked up sharply, his jaw tightening. "Gods of the sea? You mean... you believe these myths?"

Niño met his gaze, his expression serious. "These aren't just myths, Admiral. I've seen enough on this voyage to believe that there's truth in the stories. The Leviathan, the sirens, the storms—they're all connected to this route. My ancestors called it 'The Path of the Sea Gods.' It leads through waters where the boundaries between our world and theirs are thin. If we continue on this course, we will face more than just storms and monsters. We're sailing into the domain of ancient powers."

Columbus frowned, studying the symbols on the map more closely. "Why didn't you show me this sooner?"

Niño sighed, leaning back in his chair. "I didn't think it would come to this. When we set out, I believed we could navigate the waters without disturbing whatever lies beyond the surface. But the deeper we've sailed, the more the signs have shown themselves. We're not just sailing into uncharted waters—we're entering a place that was never meant to be crossed by men."

The weight of Niño's words settled heavily in the room. Columbus leaned over the map, his fingers tracing the route that Niño had laid before him. The path wound through treacherous seas, marked by symbols of warning—whirlpools, jagged rocks, and strange creatures drawn in dark ink. There were places on the map that seemed almost deliberately obscured, as if even the map's creators had been reluctant to record them in full detail.

"This is what we've been following all along," Columbus murmured, his eyes distant. "I thought we were finding a new route to the Indies, but instead... we've stumbled into something far older."

Niño nodded. "We're not the first to sail these waters. My ancestors charted this path, but few who ventured into it ever returned. Those who did came back with stories of gods that ruled the seas, creatures beyond imagining. This map was passed down as a warning, not a guide."

For a long moment, Columbus was silent, his mind racing as he processed the gravity of Niño's revelation. The events of the past few weeks suddenly took on a new, darker meaning. The sirens, the Leviathan, even the strange overcast sky—they were not random occurrences. They were part of this ancient route, a passage into a world where forces older than mankind still held sway.

"Why didn't your ancestors destroy this map?" Columbus asked finally, his voice tense. "Why did they keep it, if they knew it was so dangerous?"

"Curiosity," Niño replied, his voice soft. "The same reason we're out here now. They knew the risks, but they couldn't resist the lure of the unknown. They wanted to understand the mysteries of the sea gods, to unlock the secrets hidden in these waters. But the deeper they went, the more they realized that some things are not meant to be understood."

Columbus sat back, running a hand through his hair. He stared at the map for a long moment, then looked up at Niño, his expression hard.

"And now we're in their world."

Niño nodded. "Yes. And if we continue, the dangers will only grow. We've seen the Leviathan, but there are other things out there—things even worse. The sea gods guard this route, and they don't take kindly to intruders."

Columbus exhaled slowly, his mind weighed down by the knowledge that Niño had revealed. The path they were on was not just a route to discovery—it was a passage into a realm where ancient forces ruled, and those forces had already begun to stir.

"What do you suggest?" Columbus asked finally, his voice quiet but firm.

Niño looked down at the map, then back at Columbus. "We can still turn back. We're in dangerous waters, but it's not too late to reverse course and leave this route behind. If we press forward, we'll be challenging the very gods of the sea. The risks are unimaginable."

Columbus studied the map for a long moment, then shook his head slowly. "We've come too far. We're not turning back now. Whatever lies ahead, we'll face it. We'll find a way through."

Niño wasn't surprised by the answer. Columbus had always been driven by ambition, by the need to uncover new worlds and push beyond the boundaries of the known. But Niño couldn't help but feel a deep sense of foreboding as he looked at the path that lay ahead. The dangers were real, and the price for crossing into the realm of the sea gods would be steep.

"Then we prepare," Niño said quietly. "But know this—if we continue on this path, we are no longer sailing by the laws of men. We are entering the domain of powers far older, and far more dangerous, than anything we've ever known."

Columbus nodded, his eyes burning with determination. "We'll find a way. We always do."

Niño didn't respond. He folded the ancient map carefully and slipped it back into the folds of his cloak. He had revealed the truth to

Columbus, but in doing so, he had also acknowledged the reality they now faced.

The sea gods were watching. And as they sailed deeper into their waters, the ancient powers of the ocean would awaken.

Niño only hoped that they would be ready when the time came.

Chapter 18: Lost in the Fog

The sky had been an unrelenting gray for days, and the oppressive stillness of the sea had left the men on edge. After Niño revealed the ancient map, a new sense of dread settled over the fleet. It wasn't just the Leviathan or the sirens that haunted their minds—it was the knowledge that they were sailing deeper into waters ruled by powers older than time itself. The sea gods, Niño had said, guarded these waters, and now, with every passing hour, it felt as though the ocean itself was watching them, waiting.

On the morning of the fifth day after the Leviathan attack, something changed.

The wind, which had been gentle and erratic, suddenly stopped. The sails hung limp, and the air grew unnaturally still. The sea was like glass, reflecting the dark clouds that continued to blot out the sun. A strange, heavy quiet descended over the ships. It was as if the world had been paused, the ocean and sky holding their breath.

And then, without warning, the fog rolled in.

At first, it seemed like a normal mist—thin tendrils of white creeping across the surface of the water. But within minutes, the fog thickened, swallowing the ships in a dense, suffocating cloud. It moved quickly, wrapping around the *Santa Maria*, the *Pinta*, and the *Niña* like the fingers of some unseen force. The men shouted in alarm, scrambling to their positions as visibility dropped to near nothing. Within moments, the ships were completely engulfed, cut off from one another, lost in a sea of white.

"Drop anchor!" Columbus ordered, his voice tight with fear. "We can't risk moving in this!"

The crew obeyed, but the fog was unnerving. The dense, swirling mist seemed to muffle sound, making even the creaking of the ship's timbers sound distant and ghostly. The men stood on deck, peering into the fog, but they could see nothing beyond the rails—just an endless expanse of white, thick and impenetrable.

Niño stood at the helm, his hand gripping the wheel tightly. He had never seen fog like this before. It wasn't natural. The air was too still, too heavy, and the fog seemed to pulse with a strange, otherworldly energy, as though it were alive. He could feel it pressing against him, wrapping around his body like a damp, suffocating blanket.

"Admiral," Niño said quietly, "this is no ordinary fog. We're in dangerous waters now—this could be the work of the sea gods."

Columbus shot him a sharp glance, but he said nothing. His face was pale, his eyes wide with the same fear that had gripped the rest of the crew. They had survived the Leviathan, the sirens, and countless other dangers, but this... this was different. It wasn't a beast they could fight or a storm they could navigate through. The fog was a force of nature, an elemental power beyond their control.

"We need to stay together," Columbus said, his voice shaky but determined. "Signal the other ships. We can't lose contact."

One of the sailors ran to the bell, ringing it loudly in an attempt to signal the *Pinta* and the *Niña*, but the sound seemed to vanish into the fog, swallowed by the unnatural stillness. The crew strained their ears, hoping to hear a response, but there was nothing—no answering bell, no voices, no sounds at all. The fog had completely cut them off from the other ships.

"We've lost them," one of the sailors said, his voice barely above a whisper.

Panic began to ripple through the crew. Men moved about the deck, shouting to one another, but their voices sounded small and distant in the oppressive fog. The isolation was overwhelming, the sense of being completely alone in an endless void. It was as if the world outside the ship had ceased to exist, leaving only the *Santa Maria* and its terrified crew adrift in a sea of white.

Niño's heart pounded in his chest as he tried to stay calm. He had navigated through dangerous waters before, but this... this was different. The fog was too thick, too suffocating, and it was growing colder. He could see the fear in the men's eyes—the kind of fear that turned quickly into desperation. They had been pushed to their limits already, and now this unrelenting fog seemed like the final nail in their coffin.

"Stay calm," Niño called out, trying to keep his voice steady. "This fog will pass. We just need to wait."

But as the minutes stretched into hours, the fog showed no signs of clearing. It only grew thicker, pressing in around the ship like a living thing. The air grew colder, damp with moisture, and the crew huddled together, their breath visible in the chill. The men whispered to one another, their words filled with fear and superstition.

"I told you," one of the sailors muttered. "The sea gods don't want us here. They're punishing us for trespassing into their waters."

Another sailor nodded, his face pale. "This is their doing. The fog... it's a curse. We'll never find our way out."

Columbus, overhearing the conversation, slammed his fist down on the rail. "Enough! We're not cursed, and we're not lost. We'll find a way through this."

But even as he spoke, there was a note of doubt in his voice. He turned to Niño, his eyes filled with unspoken fear. "Do you really think this is... them?"

Niño hesitated, his gaze drifting to the ancient map hidden in his cloak. He had shown Columbus the path they were on—the route through the waters ruled by the old gods. And now, with the fog cutting them off from the world, it seemed as though the map's warnings were coming to life.

"I don't know," Niño admitted. "But this fog isn't natural. It's like the sea itself is trying to blind us, keep us from moving forward—or from turning back."

Columbus cursed under his breath, his hands gripping the rail as he stared out into the impenetrable whiteness. "We can't stay like this. We'll be sitting ducks if something attacks us again."

Niño nodded, but his mind was racing. If this fog was truly the work of the sea gods—if they had ventured too far into forbidden waters—then they were facing forces beyond their comprehension. They could wait for the fog to lift, but there was no guarantee it ever would. They were at the mercy of powers they couldn't see, couldn't fight.

And then, a sound cut through the stillness.

It was faint at first, barely audible over the creaking of the ship, but it grew louder, more distinct—a low, rumbling sound that seemed to come from the depths of the sea itself. The men froze, their eyes wide with terror. It was the same sound they had heard before the Leviathan had emerged from the deep, but this time it was different. It was more distant, more ominous, as if something far larger was stirring beneath the waves.

"Do you hear that?" one of the sailors whispered, his voice trembling.

Niño's blood ran cold as the sound grew louder, echoing through the fog. It was a warning, a signal that something ancient and powerful was moving beneath them. The fog wasn't just a barrier—it was a trap, a way to blind them, to disorient them before the next attack.

"We need to move," Niño said urgently, his voice tight with fear. "We can't stay here."

Columbus nodded, his face pale but resolute. "Raise the anchor! We need to get out of this fog before it's too late."

The men scrambled to obey, but the fog was so thick that it made every movement feel sluggish, as if they were trapped in a dream. The ship groaned as the anchor was hauled up, and the *Santa Maria* began to drift once more, its sails catching what little wind there was.

But as they moved through the fog, the eerie rumbling continued, growing louder with each passing moment. Niño's heart raced as he gripped the wheel, his eyes scanning the white void for any sign of the other ships, for any hint of what was coming.

And then, through the fog, a shadow began to emerge.

At first, it was faint, barely visible through the thick mist. But as it grew closer, its form became clearer—massive, towering, like a wall of darkness moving toward them. The men stared in horror as the shape loomed over the ship, and the rumbling grew louder, vibrating through the deck and into their bones.

"By God..." Columbus whispered, his eyes wide with fear.

The shadow grew larger, closer, until it was almost upon them. Whatever it was, it was vast—larger than the Leviathan, larger than anything they had ever seen. And it was coming for them, hidden in the fog, moving silently and swiftly through the water.

They were truly lost.

And whatever was in the fog was coming to claim them.

Chapter 19: Voices in the Water

The *Santa Maria* drifted through the thick, oppressive fog, its sails barely stirring in the stagnant air. The rumbling that had sent chills down the spines of the crew had subsided, leaving behind a heavy silence. But that silence was soon replaced by something far worse.

At first, it was barely noticeable—faint, like the distant murmur of the wind. But as the ship continued its aimless journey through the fog, the sounds became clearer. Whispers. Low, indistinct voices rising from the water itself, as though the sea was trying to speak to them. The men on deck paused, straining their ears to catch the sound, their faces pale and tight with fear.

"What is that?" one of the sailors muttered, his eyes wide as he peered over the side of the ship.

Niño stood at the helm, his heart pounding in his chest. He had heard the voices, too—soft, insidious, as if they were coming from beneath the waves, seeping up through the water and into the air. It wasn't the same as the sirens' song. This was different. Darker. More ancient. The whispers were not seductive or alluring; they were cold, detached, like the murmurs of beings that existed long before man ever set sail on the sea.

"They're coming from the water," Niño said quietly, more to himself than to anyone else.

Columbus, standing beside him, turned sharply. "What do you mean? Voices in the water? That's impossible."

Niño shook his head, his eyes scanning the swirling mist around them. "Not impossible. This is their domain, Admiral. The sea gods. These waters—they're theirs. And those voices... they're not human."

The crew, already on edge, had grown more restless with every passing moment. The whispers were growing louder now, filling the air with a strange, eerie chorus that seemed to come from all around them. The men clutched at their weapons, but there was nothing to fight. Nothing they could see. Only the voices, rising and falling like the tide, speaking in a language they couldn't understand, but somehow *felt* deep in their bones.

One of the younger sailors, a man named Tomas, stumbled toward the side of the ship, his eyes wide and unfocused. His lips moved as if he were trying to respond to the voices, though no sound came out. Niño watched him with growing concern as the sailor leaned over the rail, peering down into the dark, swirling water below.

"Tomas!" one of his crewmates called, rushing forward to pull him back. "What are you doing? Get away from the edge!"

But Tomas didn't respond. His eyes were glassy, fixed on something just beneath the surface of the water. And then, to the horror of the crew, he began to speak. His voice was low, almost a whisper, but it carried a weight that sent a chill down the spine of every man who heard it.

"They're calling me," Tomas murmured, his voice distant. "They're waiting... beneath the waves. They want us... to join them."

"Tomas, snap out of it!" the sailor beside him shouted, shaking him. "There's nothing down there! Come on, man!"

But Tomas's eyes were empty, his body swaying slightly as if he were already half gone. And then, with a sudden, violent movement, he tore himself away from his crewmate and lunged toward the rail. Before anyone could stop him, he hurled himself over the side of the ship, vanishing into the dark water below.

"Tomas!" the men shouted, rushing to the edge.

But it was too late. Tomas was gone, swallowed by the sea without a trace. A heavy, stunned silence fell over the deck as the men stared at the water, their faces pale with shock. The whispers had grown louder now, more insistent, as if the ocean itself was alive, speaking to them, drawing them in. And one by one, the men began to feel the pull. It was subtle at first, a faint tug at the edges of their minds, but it grew stronger, more seductive, as the minutes ticked by. The men's eyes darted nervously to the water, to each other, and back again. The fog pressed closer, thick and suffocating, amplifying the eerie whispers that seemed to wrap themselves around their thoughts, pulling them toward the abyss.

"It's in my head..." one sailor whispered, clutching his temples. "I can hear them... calling me."

Another man staggered back from the rail, his breath coming in ragged gasps. "We need to stop them! They... they want us to join them. We can't stay here!"

Panic began to ripple through the crew. Some tried to cover their ears, but it did nothing to block out the insidious voices. Others looked toward Niño and Columbus, desperate for orders, for something to break the grip the whispers had on their minds. But even Niño, usually calm in the face of danger, was visibly shaken.

"They are not human," Niño said softly, his eyes distant, as if he were listening to something only he could hear. "These voices... they belong to something ancient. Something older than any man or beast."

Columbus, though still trying to maintain control, was pale, his hand gripping the ship's rail tightly. "What are they?" he asked, his voice barely above a whisper. "What do they want?"

Niño turned to him, his expression grim. "They are the remnants of an ancient race, rulers of the seas before our time. The sea gods themselves. These are their voices, their warnings, echoing from the deep. They don't just want us gone, Admiral. They want to claim us. To pull us down into the depths where they dwell, to make us part of their world."

The crew, overhearing Niño's words, recoiled in fear. The whispers seemed to grow louder, more insistent, as if in response to Niño's revelation. The water lapped at the sides of the ship, dark and inviting, and the fog swirled around them like a living thing, pressing closer with every passing moment.

Suddenly, another sailor broke from the group, his face twisted in terror. "I can't take it!" he screamed. "They're in my head!"

Before anyone could stop him, he leaped overboard, vanishing into the cold, black water. His disappearance was as swift and final as Tomas's, and the remaining crew stood frozen, too afraid to move, too terrified to think.

Niño's hands clenched into fists as he fought to keep control. He could feel the whispers, too, a low, constant hum at the edge of his consciousness, pulling him toward the sea. But he resisted, gritting his teeth, forcing himself to focus on the reality of the deck beneath his feet, the creak of the wood, the chill of the fog. He wouldn't let the voices take him.

"Admiral," Niño said, his voice low but firm. "We have to act now. If we don't get out of this fog, if we don't move away from whatever's beneath us, more men will be lost. These whispers—they're not a warning. They're a trap."

Columbus, still pale and shaken, nodded slowly. "But how do we fight something we can't see?"

"We don't fight it," Niño replied. "We run. We sail as far away from here as possible, before the sea takes us all."

Columbus didn't hesitate this time. "Raise the sails!" he shouted, his voice trembling but clear. "We're getting out of here, now!"

The men moved quickly, driven by terror, their hands shaking as they worked to hoist the sails and prepare the ship to move. But even as they hurried, the whispers grew louder, more seductive, worming their way into the minds of the crew. The ocean below seemed to ripple, dark and deep, as if something was moving beneath the surface, watching, waiting.

As the *Santa Maria* began to pull away, the fog clung to them like a jealous lover, reluctant to let go. The voices continued to rise from the water, cold and ancient, promising peace, promising release—if only they would give in, if only they would let go.

But Niño stood firm at the helm, his jaw set, his eyes focused on the horizon, or what little of it he could see through the fog. He knew that if they didn't escape soon, the voices would claim them all, one by one, until there was nothing left but empty ships drifting through the fog, crewed by ghosts.

With a sudden gust of wind, the sails filled, and the *Santa Maria* lurched forward, cutting through the water with renewed speed. The fog began to thin, and the whispers—still present, still calling—grew fainter, retreating as the ship moved farther away.

As the last of the fog lifted, the men exhaled in unison, relief flooding their faces. But the memory of the whispers lingered, and the sea, though calm once more, felt more dangerous than ever.

Niño stood silently at the helm, his hands gripping the wheel. He could still hear the voices, faint now, fading into the distance. But he knew they weren't gone.

They were simply waiting for their next opportunity to strike.

Part V: The Edge of the World
Chapter 20: The Fear of No Return

The fog had lifted, but the oppressive sense of dread hung over the crew like a death shroud. The whispers that had driven men overboard still lingered in the minds of those who remained, a haunting reminder that they were sailing through waters not meant for mortal men. Each day felt longer than the last, as if time itself had slowed, trapping them in an endless, directionless journey.

The sky remained heavy with dark clouds, and the sea, though calm, felt unnaturally still. There was no wind, no movement in the air. It was as if the world around them had died, leaving only their ships and the endless, uncharted waters that stretched beyond the horizon. The men moved about their duties with hollow eyes, their once-hopeful expressions replaced by the vacant stares of men who no longer believed they would see home again.

Niño stood at the helm, his gaze fixed on the distant horizon, though there was nothing to see but the same gray expanse of water. He could feel the tension in the air, the weight of despair pressing down on the crew. They had been sailing for weeks, perhaps months—time had lost meaning—and still, there was no sign of land. No stars to guide them, no sun to warm their faces. Just the endless void of the sea, as if they had sailed beyond the reach of the world itself.

And that was what the men had begun to believe.

"They say we're sailing to the edge of the world," one of the sailors whispered to his crewmate as they worked to repair a tear in the sails. "No ships have ever returned from these waters. What if we've gone too far?"

His companion, an older, more seasoned sailor, glanced around nervously, his hands trembling as he worked. "I've heard the stories too.

Ships that sailed too far west, never to be seen again. They say the sea just drops off into nothing, into an abyss that swallows everything."

Niño overheard their conversation and clenched his jaw. He had tried to keep the crew steady, but fear had a way of spreading like a plague. The events of the past few weeks—the Leviathan, the sirens, the whispers in the water—had shaken the men's belief in their mission. Now, with no land in sight, their hope had all but crumbled.

As the day wore on, more sailors began to whisper about the abyss. Some claimed they could feel it in the air, a dark presence pulling them toward it. Others swore they had seen something at the edge of the horizon—a dark line, as if the world truly did end just beyond their reach. The more they talked, the more the fear took root, and soon, even the most level-headed men began to question whether they would ever return.

That night, as the ship drifted aimlessly on the still water, the crew gathered in small groups, huddled together against the cold. The wind had died again, and the ship barely moved. The sky was a deep, featureless black, and the air was thick with the smell of salt and damp wood. There was no sound but the creaking of the ship and the soft murmur of the waves.

"They're right, you know," a sailor named Juan muttered, his voice trembling as he stared out at the water. "We're sailing to the end of the world. I can feel it."

Another sailor, Diego, scoffed, though his voice lacked conviction. "There's no end of the world, Juan. The sea just goes on, that's all."

"No," Juan insisted, his eyes wide and haunted. "It's not just the sea. It's the abyss. I saw it today, in the distance. A line of darkness, like the edge of the earth itself. We're being pulled toward it."

Several of the other men nodded in agreement, their faces pale and anxious. Niño, standing nearby, listened quietly, his heart sinking. The fear was spreading faster than he had anticipated. He knew he had to act, had to say something to keep the crew from descending into full-blown panic.

But what could he say? He had seen the same emptiness stretching before them, felt the same creeping dread that they were sailing toward something they couldn't escape. Even he, the man who had navigated the most treacherous waters, was beginning to doubt their course.

As Niño moved toward the men, Columbus emerged from his quarters, his face shadowed and gaunt. He had been wrestling with his own demons, trying to maintain control over the situation, but even he could not hide the despair that had settled over him like a heavy cloak.

"The abyss is just a story," Columbus said, his voice loud enough to reach the men. "There's no edge of the world. We're still on course, and we will find land. We've faced worse than this—storms, monsters—and we've survived. We will survive this too."

The men looked at him, but their eyes held no spark of belief. The weight of the journey, the endless sea, and the strange, unnatural phenomena they had encountered had drained them of hope. They were no longer the eager sailors who had set out from Spain with dreams of gold and glory. Now, they were broken men, lost in a world that no longer made sense.

"How can you be sure?" one of the men asked, his voice thin and weak. "How can you know we'll find land? We've been sailing for so long, and all we've seen is this... nothing."

Columbus faltered for a moment, but then Niño stepped forward, his voice calm and steady. "We're not lost. The sea is testing us, yes. It's trying to break us. But we are sailors. We were born to navigate these waters, to push beyond what is known. There is no abyss, no edge of the world. These are just tales born of fear, and fear is the greatest enemy we face now."

The men listened, their eyes fixed on Niño. He spoke with a conviction that Columbus had begun to lose, and for a moment, a flicker of hope returned to their faces.

"But what if the stories are true?" Diego asked quietly. "What if we've sailed too far? What if there's no way back?"

Niño met his gaze, his expression firm. "Then we keep sailing. We've come this far, and we will find our way. If there is an abyss, we will steer clear of it. But giving in to fear will only lead us into darkness."

For a long moment, there was silence. The men exchanged uneasy glances, their fear not entirely dispelled but tempered by Niño's words. They returned to their duties, though their movements were slow, hesitant, as if they were still haunted by the idea of the abyss waiting for them at the edge of the world.

As the night wore on, the ship continued its slow, drifting course, the sails hanging limp in the still air. The men slept fitfully, their dreams filled with images of dark waters, of unseen forces pulling them into the depths.

Niño remained awake, standing at the helm, his eyes scanning the horizon. He had reassured the crew, but deep down, he could not shake the feeling that they were indeed being drawn toward something—something ancient and vast, waiting for them in the darkest part of the ocean.

And as the first light of dawn crept across the sky, casting the sea in shades of gray, Niño thought he saw it—just for a moment, on the distant horizon.

A line of darkness, faint but unmistakable, where the sea seemed to fall away into nothing.

The abyss.

Niño blinked, and the line was gone, swallowed by the morning mist.

But the fear remained.

Chapter 21: An Unseen Force

The next morning brought little comfort to the weary crew of the *Santa Maria*. The fog had dissipated, but the sea remained eerily calm, almost too calm. The sky was a dull, featureless gray, and the wind, though present, felt wrong—cold and faint, as if it carried no energy. It barely stirred the sails, and the ship drifted more than it sailed, its movements slow and lethargic.

Columbus paced the deck, his face drawn and gaunt. The events of the past few days—the fog, the whispers, the sailors who had thrown themselves into the sea—had rattled him deeply. The men were on edge, their spirits crushed by the endless, unchanging horizon and the growing sense that they were being lured into some kind of trap. It was as if the sea itself had conspired against them, drawing them ever deeper into its clutches.

And now, as Columbus gazed out over the water, a new and unsettling phenomenon began to unfold.

The waves, which had been gently lapping at the hull, suddenly shifted direction. They no longer followed the wind, which blew faintly from the east, but moved against it, flowing unnaturally toward the west. The sea undulated in strange, rhythmic patterns, as if some unseen force beneath the surface was controlling its movements. The men who had been working on the deck stopped and stared, their eyes wide with disbelief.

"What's happening?" one of the sailors whispered, his voice trembling. "Why is the sea moving like that?"

Niño, standing at the helm, narrowed his eyes as he watched the waves. It was as if the ocean had come alive, acting under the influence of something beyond the natural world. He had seen strange currents before, had navigated dangerous waters where the winds and tides seemed at odds, but this was different. The water was behaving with purpose, as though it were being guided.

"We're not alone," Niño muttered to himself, his gaze fixed on the shimmering surface of the water.

Columbus approached him, his face pale. "What do you make of it, Niño? The sea... it's moving against the wind."

Niño didn't answer immediately. Instead, he leaned over the rail, studying the water with growing unease. The waves were small but steady, all flowing in the same unnatural direction. And as he watched, he noticed something else—something that made his heart skip a beat.

The water, normally dark and opaque, began to shimmer. It caught the dull light of the sky, reflecting it back like polished silver. The surface gleamed with an almost metallic sheen, as if the ocean had been transformed into liquid metal. The sight was mesmerizing, beautiful in a way that felt entirely wrong. It was as if the sea had become something otherworldly, a mirror of another reality just beneath the surface.

"I don't like this," Niño said quietly. "The sea shouldn't be behaving like this. There's something... unnatural about it."

Columbus stared at the shimmering water, his brow furrowed. "Do you think it's the sea gods again? The forces your ancestors spoke of?"

Niño hesitated, his mind racing. He had been thinking the same thing. The ancient map, passed down through his family, had warned of waters ruled by beings older than time itself, gods that controlled the seas and all that dwelled within them. And now, with the strange behavior of the waves and the shimmering surface, it felt as though they had entered the domain of those very gods.

"I don't know," Niño finally replied, though he could feel the truth lurking at the edge of his mind. "But whatever it is, we're being watched. I can feel it."

Columbus nodded grimly. "We need to keep the men calm. They've already seen too much—they're on the verge of breaking."

Niño glanced at the crew. The sailors were huddled together, whispering in hushed tones, their eyes darting nervously between the water and the horizon. They had seen the strange behavior of the sea, too, and it was clear that they were unsettled. Some of them clutched their rosaries, muttering prayers under their breath, while others simply stared at the water, as if expecting something terrible to rise from the depths.

As the day wore on, the unnatural phenomena continued. The waves moved in ways that defied logic, shifting directions with no regard for the wind. Sometimes they rippled outward in perfect concentric circles, as though a great stone had been dropped into the center of the ocean. Other times, the water would flatten completely, becoming still as glass before suddenly surging upward in strange, spiraling columns that disappeared just as quickly.

And always, the shimmering silver gleam persisted, casting a strange, ethereal light over the ship and its surroundings. The men began to mutter more openly now, their voices tinged with fear.

"The sea's cursed," one sailor said, his voice trembling. "We've angered something—something old. It's watching us."

"Maybe it's the abyss," another whispered. "Maybe we've sailed too far, and the sea's going to swallow us whole."

Niño clenched his fists, trying to keep his own fear in check. He could feel it too—an unseen presence, something vast and ancient, watching them from beneath the waves. It was as if the sea itself was alive, aware of their intrusion, and was toying with them, testing their resolve. The shimmering surface and the unnatural waves were just the beginning, a warning of something far more dangerous lurking just out of sight.

That night, as the ship drifted through the unnaturally calm waters, Columbus called for a meeting in his quarters. Niño, along with the ship's officers, gathered around the small table where the ancient map lay unfurled. The flickering light of a lantern cast deep shadows across the room, and the tension was palpable.

"We need to talk about what's happening out there," Columbus said, his voice low but steady. "The sea is behaving in ways none of us can explain, and the men are losing hope. They believe we're cursed."

Niño nodded. "They're not entirely wrong. This place... these waters... they're not like anything we've seen before. The sea gods, if that's what they are, are watching us. They control these waters, and they're making sure we know it."

One of the officers, a grizzled sailor named Fernandez, frowned. "So what do we do? We can't just turn back—there's no wind to carry us. And if we keep sailing, we could be heading straight into whatever's waiting for us."

Columbus rubbed his temples, his frustration evident. "We can't stay here. Whatever's controlling the sea, we need to keep moving. We need to find a way out of this."

"But what if there is no way out?" Fernandez muttered darkly. "What if this is the end of the world, like the men say? What if we're sailing straight into the abyss?"

Niño's gaze flicked to the map, the ancient chart that had led them this far. The path they had followed had brought them deep into the heart of these dangerous waters, and now it seemed as though the sea itself had come alive to block their way. He thought of the shimmering water, the strange behavior of the waves, and the growing sense that they were being watched by something vast and unknowable.

"We keep sailing," Niño said finally, his voice quiet but firm. "We don't stop. Whatever is out there, whatever is watching us, it's testing us. If we falter, if we give in to fear, we'll be lost. But if we keep moving, we might find a way through."

Columbus nodded, though there was doubt in his eyes. "And if we don't?"

Niño looked at him, his face grim. "Then we face whatever's waiting for us. But we do it on our terms."

As the meeting ended and the men returned to their stations, the ship continued its slow journey through the shimmering, unnatural sea. The night was still, the air heavy with the feeling of being watched. And though the men worked quietly, their minds were consumed by the fear of what lay ahead.

The sea had become something else, something alive. And whatever was watching them from the depths was waiting for the right moment to strike.

Chapter 22: The Navigator's Oath

The *Santa Maria* drifted through the unnatural sea, its crew quiet and somber as they worked. The shimmering silver water glistened under the pale, featureless sky, reflecting an eerie light that seemed to make time itself feel suspended. The strange behavior of the sea had everyone on edge, but something more insidious was beginning to creep through the hearts of the men—doubt. It gnawed at their minds, whispering that they might never find their way back, that they had ventured too far into the unknown, led by a captain whose dream of discovery had turned into a nightmare.

Niño, standing at the helm, felt the weight of responsibility press down on him more heavily than ever. He had always prided himself on being a skilled navigator, on reading the stars and guiding ships safely through even the most treacherous waters. But now, with no stars to guide them, with the sea behaving in ways that defied nature, he found himself questioning not just his skills, but his purpose.

Late in the evening, as the ship moved slowly across the shimmering water, Columbus approached Niño. The captain's face was worn, his once-burning ambition now dulled by the strange and terrifying events that had befallen them. He leaned against the rail beside Niño, gazing out at the horizon where the sea and sky seemed to blur into one endless, featureless void.

"We're being tested," Columbus said quietly, his voice laced with exhaustion. "I can feel it. The men are losing hope, and if we don't find land soon, we might lose more than just our way."

Niño didn't respond immediately. He watched the strange, shimmering water ripple beneath the ship, the reflection of the moonless sky turning the sea into something otherworldly. He had felt the same thing—an unseen force, testing their resolve, watching their every move. But there was something deeper, something he had known for a long time, and now, with the crew on the brink of despair, he could no longer keep it to himself.

"Admiral," Niño said softly, his voice barely audible above the gentle lapping of the waves, "there's something I need to tell you. Something I should have told you from the beginning."

Columbus turned to look at him, his brow furrowed. "What is it?"

Niño took a deep breath, the weight of his secret pressing heavily on his chest. For years, he had carried the knowledge of his heritage, of the legacy passed down through his family, but he had always kept it hidden. The world of European exploration was not kind to those who did not fit neatly into its narrative, and Niño's ancestors were not part of the accepted history. But now, with the crew's fate hanging in the balance, he could no longer stay silent.

"My ancestors," Niño began, his voice steady but filled with a quiet intensity, "came from a land beyond the seas. A place forgotten by time, known only to a few who still carry the knowledge. They were navigators, explorers who sailed these waters long before any European set out to chart the oceans. The map I showed you—the one that led us here—it was passed down through my family for generations."

Columbus's eyes widened in surprise, but he remained silent, listening intently.

"They were part of an ancient people," Niño continued, "who knew the seas like no one else. They spoke of lands beyond the horizon, places where the stars were different, where the ocean itself held secrets too dangerous for most to understand. My ancestors believed that the sea was alive, that it had its own will, and that those who sailed too far would encounter forces beyond human comprehension."

Columbus's expression hardened. "You're saying your ancestors knew of these waters? That they had been here before?"

Niño nodded. "Yes. The map we've been following was their creation, a record of their journey into these unknown seas. But it wasn't just a map—it was a warning. A path to a place long forgotten, a place where the sea gods still hold power. My family kept it hidden for centuries, passing it down only to those who understood the risks. I was taught never to use it, never to follow the path. But when you spoke of your vision, of finding a new route to the Indies, I believed that perhaps this was the moment. Perhaps I was meant to guide us to this place."

Columbus stared at Niño, his eyes dark with a mix of curiosity and disbelief. "You've known all along that we were sailing into dangerous waters, and you didn't say anything?"

"I didn't know for sure," Niño said, his voice strained. "I thought... I hoped... that we could navigate through these waters without disturbing the forces that dwell here. But now, with everything we've encountered—the Leviathan, the whispers, the strange behavior of the sea—it's clear that we've ventured too far. The map wasn't just a guide; it was a key, unlocking something ancient and powerful."

Columbus clenched his fists, his frustration boiling over. "And now we're trapped in it. We're lost, with no way forward and no way back."

Niño shook his head. "We're not lost. But we are being tested. My ancestors believed that only those who truly understood the sea could navigate these waters and survive. They spoke of an oath, a promise made to the sea gods, to respect their domain. If we can earn their favor, if we can prove ourselves worthy, we may still find a way through."

Columbus frowned, his skepticism clear. "And how do we do that? How do we prove ourselves to gods we can't see, gods that seem determined to destroy us?"

Niño's gaze shifted to the horizon, where the silver shimmer of the sea seemed to glow faintly in the darkness. "We don't fight them. We don't challenge them. We surrender to the sea's will, let it guide us. My ancestors believed that the sea itself would reveal the path to those who showed respect and understanding. If we are to survive, we must stop trying to control it and start listening to it."

Columbus stared at Niño for a long moment, his jaw clenched in frustration. He had spent his life charting courses, navigating by the stars, always in control of his destiny. But now, in this place where the natural laws no longer seemed to apply, he found himself at a loss. The idea of surrendering to forces he couldn't understand or predict went against everything he had ever believed. But deep down, he knew Niño was right. The sea wasn't just water and waves—it was something more, something ancient and alive.

"And if we don't?" Columbus asked quietly. "If we refuse to surrender?"

Niño's eyes were filled with the weight of his ancestors' knowledge, of the countless generations who had sailed these waters and either returned with tales of wonder or disappeared without a trace.

"Then the sea will claim us," Niño said softly. "Just like it has claimed those who came before."

For a long time, neither man spoke. The ship creaked softly beneath them, the strange, shimmering water reflecting the pale light of the night sky. Columbus turned his gaze to the horizon, where the sea stretched out in all directions, endless and unknowable.

"We keep sailing," Columbus said finally, his voice quiet but resolute. "We listen to the sea. And we hope that it leads us somewhere we can survive."

Niño nodded, feeling the weight of his oath settle over him. He had taken on the responsibility of guiding this crew into the unknown, following the path of his ancestors, and now they were at the mercy of the ancient forces that ruled these waters.

As the night wore on and the ship drifted across the shimmering sea, Niño silently swore that he would do everything in his power to guide them through the dangers ahead. But he knew that in the end, their fate rested not in his hands, but in the will of the sea gods.

And whatever trial awaited them next, Niño would face it with the knowledge that he was fulfilling the oath his ancestors had made long ago—to respect the sea, to follow its path, and to trust in its power.

But deep within him, a darker thought lingered. What if the path they were on was not one of survival, but of sacrifice? What if the sea had chosen them not as explorers, but as an offering to the forgotten gods who ruled its depths?

Chapter 23: The Kraken's Wrath

The eerie calm that had settled over the sea was thick with tension, like the air before a storm. The strange, shimmering water continued to ripple unnaturally beneath the ships, but now, every creak of the hull and every sigh of wind seemed to carry the weight of something far more sinister. The crew moved quietly, their eyes constantly scanning the horizon, expecting the next horror to emerge from the depths at any moment.

Niño stood at the helm, his grip tight on the wheel as he watched the waters with growing unease. The sea had grown unnaturally still, and though the wind remained faint, the sails of the *Santa Maria* barely fluttered. The strange behavior of the ocean—the shimmering silver surface, the waves moving against the wind—had left everyone on edge. But Niño sensed that something worse was coming. There was a weight in the air, a pressure that made it hard to breathe, as if the ocean itself was holding its breath, waiting for the moment to strike.

It came without warning.

A sudden, violent surge in the water sent the *Santa Maria* rocking violently, throwing several sailors off their feet. The surface of the sea rippled and churned, darkening as though something enormous was rising from below. Shouts erupted from the men on deck as they scrambled to regain their footing, their eyes wide with fear.

"By God, what is it this time?" one of the sailors cried, staring out at the water with a look of terror.

Before anyone could answer, the sea beneath them seemed to explode. From the depths, a massive, writhing mass of tentacles broke the surface, each one thicker than the ship's masts and covered in slimy, glistening suckers. The monstrous limbs shot up into the air with terrifying speed, reaching toward the sky before crashing down toward the ships with a force that shook the very ocean around them.

"The Kraken!" someone screamed, and panic erupted across the deck.

The creature was unlike anything they had ever seen—a monstrous Kraken, its enormous body hidden beneath the surface, with only its massive, writhing tentacles visible above the waves. The beast's sheer size dwarfed the fleet, its limbs stretching out in all directions, wrapping around the ships as if they were mere toys.

"All hands to battle stations!" Columbus shouted, his voice barely audible over the roar of the sea and the crashing of the tentacles.

Niño's heart raced as he watched the Kraken's monstrous limbs rise and fall, each one capable of crushing the ships or dragging them under in a matter of seconds. The crew, though terrified, rushed to arm themselves, manning the cannons and readying whatever weapons they could find. But Niño knew that the cannons would do little against a creature of this size. The Kraken was no ordinary beast—it was a force of nature, a monster from the depths, and its wrath was now fully unleashed.

One of the Kraken's tentacles slammed down onto the deck of the *Niña*, wrapping around the ship with a sickening crunch of wood and rigging. The crew aboard screamed as the ship tilted dangerously, the tentacle squeezing tighter, threatening to snap the vessel in half.

"We're being pulled under!" one of the sailors shouted, his voice filled with desperation.

Columbus turned to Niño, his face pale but determined. "We have to break free! Aim for the eyes—if we can wound it, we might have a chance!"

Niño nodded, though he knew the odds were slim. The Kraken was too large, too powerful. But they had no other choice. If they didn't fight back, the beast would drag them all into the depths, one ship at a time.

"Ready the cannons!" Niño shouted to the men. "Aim for where the tentacles meet the water!"

The cannons roared to life, firing round after round into the Kraken's writhing limbs. The shots hit the thick, rubbery flesh of the tentacles, sending sprays of seawater and blood into the air, but the creature barely seemed to notice. Its tentacles continued to thrash wildly, slamming into the ships with devastating force.

The *Pinta* was the next to be struck. A tentacle lashed out from the depths, wrapping around the stern of the ship and pulling it down into the water. The men aboard scrambled to cut the ropes and free the sails, but the Kraken's grip was relentless. The ship groaned under the pressure, tilting dangerously as the beast began to drag it beneath the waves.

"We're going down!" one of the officers on the *Pinta* shouted, his voice lost in the chaos.

Niño watched in horror as the *Pinta* was pulled lower into the water, the Kraken's tentacle tightening its grip. He turned to Columbus, his voice urgent. "We need to cut the lines! If we don't break free, we'll all be dragged under!"

Columbus nodded, his expression grim. "Do it! Cut the ropes!"

The men rushed to sever the lines connecting the ships, hoping to free themselves from the Kraken's grasp. Axes and knives flashed as they hacked away at the ropes, but the Kraken's tentacles continued to lash out, striking the ships with terrifying speed and power.

Another cannon fired, and this time the shot hit true—one of the Kraken's eyes, a massive, glowing orb that had briefly surfaced above the water. The creature let out a deafening roar, its entire body convulsing in pain. The tentacle wrapped around the *Pinta* loosened, and for a brief moment, it seemed as though they might be able to escape.

But then, with a sudden, violent surge, the Kraken reared back, pulling its massive body higher out of the water. The sea around it churned wildly, waves crashing against the sides of the ships as the creature prepared to strike again. Its tentacles flailed, and one of them shot toward the *Santa Maria*, wrapping around the hull with crushing force.

The ship groaned under the pressure, the wood splintering and cracking as the Kraken squeezed tighter. Niño felt the deck tilt beneath him, and he grabbed onto the wheel for support. The ship was being pulled under, just like the *Pinta*, and there was nothing they could do to stop it.

"We're sinking!" a sailor screamed, his voice filled with terror.

"Hold on!" Niño shouted, but even as the words left his mouth, he knew it might be too late.

The Kraken's tentacle lifted the *Santa Maria* partially out of the water, the ship groaning under the strain as men were thrown from the deck into the churning sea below. The ship creaked and shuddered, and Niño could feel the Kraken's immense power in every movement.

Desperation took hold. "Fire the cannons!" Niño shouted, his voice barely audible over the chaos. "Hit the tentacle, now!"

The cannons roared to life again, firing point-blank into the Kraken's massive limb. The shots ripped through the thick flesh, sending black blood spraying into the air. The Kraken let out another ear-splitting roar, and its grip on the *Santa Maria* loosened just enough for the ship to slip back into the water with a tremendous splash.

Niño clung to the wheel, his heart racing as the ship rocked violently. They had survived, but the Kraken was far from defeated. Its tentacles still lashed out from the depths, and its fury seemed to know no bounds.

"We can't kill it," Niño said breathlessly to Columbus, who was gripping the rail with white knuckles. "We have to find a way to escape."

Columbus nodded, his face grim. "We need more wind. We need to move, now, before it strikes again."

As if in response to their desperate pleas, a sudden gust of wind swept across the sea, filling the sails and propelling the *Santa Maria* forward. The Kraken roared once more, its tentacles thrashing as the ship began to pull away from its grasp. The men worked frantically to keep the ship moving, but the beast was relentless, pursuing them with terrifying speed.

With one last effort, Niño turned the wheel hard, steering the ship into the wind. The *Santa Maria* surged forward, breaking free of the Kraken's reach. Behind them, the sea churned and frothed as the Kraken's massive body disappeared back into the depths, its roar echoing across the ocean.

For a moment, there was silence.

The crew, battered and bruised, stood in stunned disbelief. They had survived the Kraken's wrath, but the toll had been devastating. The *Pinta* was gone, dragged beneath the waves, and the *Santa Maria* was badly damaged, its hull splintered and leaking water.

Niño leaned heavily on the wheel, his breath coming in ragged gasps. He had never faced anything like the Kraken, and the knowledge that the sea still held such horrors filled him with a deep, unsettling dread.

Columbus, pale and shaken, looked out over the water where the Kraken had disappeared. "We can't survive another attack like that," he said quietly.

Niño nodded, his voice grim. "We won't have to. We've entered the heart of the sea gods' domain. This is just the beginning."

Chapter 24: Into the Maelstrom

The crew of the *Santa Maria* was still reeling from the Kraken's attack, their faces gaunt and hollow, their spirits battered. The relentless forces of the sea had driven them to the brink of exhaustion, and the loss of the *Pinta*, dragged beneath the waves by the monstrous beast, weighed heavily on their hearts. The ship, now barely holding together, creaked with every movement as the men worked to patch the gaping wounds in the hull, their hands trembling with the knowledge that they were being hunted by forces beyond their understanding.

But Niño, standing at the helm, knew that something even more terrifying lay ahead. The Kraken had been a warning, a test, but the true trial was still to come. He could feel it in the air, in the way the wind tugged at the sails, and in the deep, unsettling rumble that had begun to rise from the ocean beneath them.

"Admiral," Niño said, his voice low but steady, "we're not done yet. The sea isn't finished with us."

Columbus, who had been pacing the deck, turned to him with a look of grim determination. "What do you mean? We survived the Kraken. What more could there be?"

Before Niño could respond, a distant roar filled the air, growing louder with each passing second. The crew froze, their eyes wide with fear as they scanned the horizon for the source of the sound. It was a deep, thundering noise, like the crash of a thousand waves breaking all at once, but there was no storm in sight. The sea remained unnervingly calm, its surface shimmering like liquid silver.

Then, suddenly, the horizon began to shift.

At first, it was subtle—a dark line, barely visible in the distance, where the sea seemed to fold in on itself. But as the fleet sailed closer, the line widened, revealing a massive, swirling vortex, its center an impenetrable black hole that seemed to devour the ocean around it.

The water spiraled downward into the vortex with incredible force, creating a roaring maelstrom that stretched for miles in every direction.

The men gasped in horror, their hands gripping the rails of the ship as they stared into the churning abyss. The swirling water moved faster than any current they had ever seen, pulling everything toward its dark center with terrifying speed. It was as if the sea itself had opened a gaping mouth, ready to consume them.

"The maelstrom," Columbus whispered, his face pale with dread. "We'll be torn apart."

Panic swept through the crew like wildfire. Men scrambled to secure the sails, shouting orders that were lost in the roar of the vortex. The ships lurched dangerously as they were pulled toward the edge of the maelstrom, the water dragging them inexorably closer to the swirling abyss. The *Santa Maria* tilted to one side, its hull creaking ominously as the force of the vortex took hold.

"Niño!" Columbus shouted, his voice barely audible over the roar. "What do we do?"

Niño's mind raced. The maelstrom was too powerful to avoid—it was pulling them in, dragging them toward the center with a force they couldn't escape. But deep within him, Niño felt something stirring, an ancient knowledge passed down through his bloodline. The stories of his ancestors, the ancient navigators who had sailed these very waters, came rushing back to him.

"There's a way through!" Niño shouted back, his voice filled with urgency. "If we can reach the eye of the maelstrom—the calm at its center—we might find a passage through."

Columbus stared at him in disbelief. "The center? Are you mad? That's suicide!"

"No," Niño insisted, his grip tightening on the wheel. "The sea gods control these waters. This vortex isn't just a trap—it's a gateway. My ancestors spoke of it, a passage to the other side, beyond the world we know. If we can reach the eye, we'll survive."

Columbus hesitated, but there was no time to argue. The fleet was being pulled closer to the edge of the maelstrom with every passing moment, the ships rocking violently as they fought against the current. The roaring water surged around them, and the men struggled to keep their balance as the *Santa Maria* was dragged toward the abyss.

"Do it!" Columbus shouted, his voice filled with desperation. "Get us to the center!"

Niño nodded and turned the wheel, steering the ship directly toward the heart of the maelstrom. The other ships followed, their captains trusting in Niño's instincts, even as the vortex loomed larger, its dark center yawning before them like the maw of some ancient, hungry beast.

The wind howled as the ships were pulled deeper into the swirling current. The water roared around them, the force of the maelstrom threatening to tear the ships apart at any moment. Men clung to the rigging and lashed themselves to the masts, their faces pale with terror as the ships hurtled toward the black center of the vortex.

The *Santa Maria* groaned under the strain, its timbers creaking and splintering as it was dragged into the spinning abyss. Niño's hands were steady on the wheel, his eyes fixed on the center of the maelstrom. He could feel the pull of the sea gods, the ancient forces that controlled these waters, guiding him toward the heart of the storm.

"Hold steady!" Niño shouted to the crew. "We're almost there!"

The ship lurched violently as it crossed the edge of the maelstrom, the water swirling around them at a dizzying speed. The men held on for dear life as the ship was tossed about like a leaf in a storm, but Niño kept his focus on the eye of the vortex—the small, calm center that lay at the heart of the chaos.

For what felt like an eternity, the *Santa Maria* spun wildly in the grip of the maelstrom. The water roared in their ears, and the ship's hull groaned under the immense pressure. But slowly, miraculously, the ship began to level out, the spinning motion growing less violent as they neared the center.

And then, suddenly, everything went quiet.

The *Santa Maria* drifted into the eye of the maelstrom, a calm, eerily still place surrounded by the swirling chaos of the vortex. The water here was smooth, untouched by the violent currents that raged just beyond the edge. The sky above was a deep, starless black, and the air was heavy with an unnatural stillness.

The crew, battered and bruised, looked around in stunned silence. They had made it. They were in the heart of the maelstrom.

Columbus stood beside Niño, his eyes wide with disbelief. "How... how did you know?"

Niño didn't answer immediately. He stared out at the calm water around them, his mind racing. The stories of his ancestors had been right—the maelstrom wasn't just a death trap, but a gateway. A passage to somewhere beyond the known world. But where did it lead?

"We're not finished yet," Niño said quietly. "This is only the beginning."

Before Columbus could respond, a deep rumble echoed from beneath the water, sending ripples across the smooth surface. The men tensed, their eyes darting to the water as the rumble grew louder, more insistent.

And then, from the depths of the maelstrom, something began to rise.

Niño's heart pounded in his chest as he watched the water churn and bubble. Whatever was coming, it was massive, far larger than the Kraken, far older than any beast they had encountered. The sea gods were not done with them yet.

And Niño knew, in that moment, that they were about to face their greatest trial.

The passage beyond the world they knew awaited them—but first, they would have to survive the wrath of the sea gods.

Part VI: Revelation and Redemption
Chapter 25: The Hidden Continent

The calm in the eye of the maelstrom had been short-lived. After the mysterious rumbling from beneath the waters, the *Santa Maria* had been tossed violently one last time before the vortex finally released its grip. The ship groaned and splintered, but it held together, as if spared by the sea gods at the last moment. When the swirling chaos of the maelstrom faded into the distance, the crew found themselves in an entirely new place—an eerie, otherworldly calm stretched across the sea.

For the first time in what felt like an eternity, the sun broke through the thick clouds above, casting a golden light over the water. The men blinked in disbelief, their eyes adjusting to the sudden brightness. The oppressive gloom that had hung over them for so long was gone, replaced by a sense of awe and confusion.

Niño stood at the helm, his grip still tight on the wheel, but his heart was lighter than it had been in days. They had made it. Somehow, through the Kraken, the whispers, and the maelstrom, they had survived. But as the mist began to clear and the horizon opened up before them, it became clear that they had arrived somewhere unlike anything they had ever seen before.

Ahead of them, rising from the sea like a dream made real, was a massive landmass—an island or perhaps a hidden continent, surrounded by jagged cliffs and dense, unfamiliar greenery. The cliffs were high and imposing, covered in strange, colorful moss that glowed faintly in the sunlight. Beyond the cliffs, towering trees stretched toward the sky, their trunks twisted in impossible shapes and their leaves a deep shade of emerald, unlike anything found in the known world.

The waters around the island shimmered with a strange, iridescent quality, reflecting the vibrant colors of the landscape. It was as if the sea itself had changed here, becoming something more alive, more magical. The island exuded an energy that was both beautiful and dangerous, a place where the natural world seemed to merge with something far more ancient and mysterious.

Columbus, standing beside Niño, stared in awe. "What is this place?" he asked, his voice filled with wonder and disbelief.

"I don't know," Niño replied, his voice barely above a whisper. "But this is no ordinary land. We've crossed into something... beyond what we know."

The crew, still shaken but alive, gathered at the rails, their eyes wide with amazement. They had heard stories of uncharted islands, lands filled with gold and riches, but this was something else entirely. This place felt untouched by time, as if it had been hidden from the rest of the world for centuries, perhaps even millennia.

One of the sailors, his voice trembling with excitement, pointed toward the cliffs. "Look! There's a beach. We can land there."

Indeed, a narrow strip of beach stretched out at the base of the cliffs, where the turquoise water lapped gently against the sand. The beach was unlike any they had seen before, with sand that sparkled like crushed gemstones and strange, iridescent shells scattered along the shore. Beyond the beach, a steep path led up into the dense jungle that covered the island.

"Prepare to make landfall," Columbus ordered, his voice regaining some of its former authority. "We need to know what this place is. If this is truly a new land, we'll be the first to claim it."

The men scrambled into action, their earlier fear replaced by a renewed sense of purpose. The ships, battered and bruised, moved slowly toward the beach, their hulls creaking as they drew closer to the strange, uncharted shore. As they neared the island, the shimmering water seemed to glow even brighter, casting an ethereal light over the deck.

As soon as the *Santa Maria* touched the shore, the men lowered the anchor, and Columbus, Niño, and a small group of sailors disembarked, stepping cautiously onto the glittering sand. The air was thick with the scent of salt and strange, sweet-smelling flowers that bloomed in the jungle beyond. The sounds of the island—the rustle of leaves, the distant cries of unfamiliar creatures—were like nothing they had ever heard before.

Niño crouched down, running his fingers through the sand. It was soft and cool, shimmering with a strange, pearlescent quality. He picked up a shell, its surface smooth and iridescent, reflecting the colors of the jungle behind them.

"This place..." Niño murmured. "It feels alive, like the land itself is watching us."

Columbus nodded, though his eyes were fixed on the dense foliage ahead. "We'll need to explore further. Whatever this place is, it holds secrets. And I intend to uncover them."

The men began to move inland, following the narrow path that led up from the beach and into the jungle. As they stepped into the shade of the towering trees, they were struck by the sheer scale of the flora. The trees were massive, their trunks twisted and gnarled, with roots that seemed to burrow deep into the earth like the veins of some ancient being. The leaves, a deep, emerald green, glowed faintly in the sunlight, casting strange, dappled patterns on the forest floor.

The air was thick with humidity, but it carried a strange, intoxicating scent—a mix of sweet flowers and earthy moss. The deeper they ventured into the jungle, the more the land around them seemed to hum with life. Strange plants grew along the path, their leaves pulsing with light, and flowers bloomed in impossible shapes and colors.

"This is no ordinary island," one of the sailors muttered, his voice tinged with awe. "It's like... it's like something from a dream."

Suddenly, a loud screech echoed through the jungle, followed by the rustling of leaves. The men froze, their hands instinctively reaching for their weapons. From the trees above, a group of strange, bird-like creatures swooped down, their wings shimmering with iridescent colors. They were unlike any birds the men had ever seen—larger, with elongated beaks and feathers that glowed with an almost metallic sheen.

The creatures screeched again, circling the group before disappearing back into the canopy above. The men stared after them, their hearts racing.

"What kind of creatures live here?" one of the sailors asked nervously.

Niño looked around, his eyes scanning the trees and the dense underbrush. He felt the same strange energy he had felt when they had first approached the island—a presence, as if the land itself was aware of their arrival.

"There's more here than meets the eye," Niño said quietly. "We've stepped into a world beyond our own."

As they ventured deeper into the jungle, the men began to notice more strange and wondrous things. Plants that seemed to move on their own, shifting and turning toward the sun. Flowers that bloomed in the shape of stars, their petals glowing faintly in the dim light. The air buzzed with the sounds of life—birds, insects, and creatures that defied explanation.

But there was something else, too—a feeling of being watched. The men could sense it, a quiet presence lurking just beyond their sight. The jungle, as beautiful and strange as it was, held secrets, and Niño knew that they had only just begun to uncover them.

As the group pressed on, they reached a clearing in the heart of the jungle. At the center of the clearing stood a massive stone structure, half-covered in vines and moss. It was ancient, its surface worn and cracked, but it was unmistakably man-made. Strange symbols were carved into the stone—symbols that Niño recognized from the ancient map passed down through his family.

Columbus stepped forward, his eyes wide with wonder. "What is this place?" he whispered.

Niño stared at the stone structure, his heart pounding. The hidden continent they had discovered was far more than just an uncharted island. This was a place long forgotten, a place where the ancient sea gods had once ruled, and where their influence still lingered.

"We've found something beyond our world," Niño said, his voice filled with awe. "This is the land my ancestors spoke of. A place lost to time."

As the men stood in the shadow of the ancient stone, they knew they had crossed into a realm that had been waiting for them—perhaps even calling them—since the beginning of their journey.

But what secrets the island held, and what dangers lay ahead, remained unknown. The land itself seemed to breathe with life, and Niño could feel the eyes of the island upon them.

Their journey was far from over.

Chapter 26: Lost Souls of the Sea

The discovery of the ancient stone structure had stirred a deep sense of awe and unease among the crew of the *Santa Maria*. The strange island, with its alien flora and otherworldly creatures, felt like a place caught between worlds, both enchanting and dangerous. Yet, there was something else in the air now—a sense of foreboding that none of the men could shake. It was as if the land itself held secrets far darker than they could imagine.

After examining the stone structure, Columbus and Niño led a small group deeper into the jungle, driven by a mixture of curiosity and dread. The carvings on the structure seemed to match the symbols from the ancient map Niño had carried, confirming that they had reached a place beyond the known world—an island that had been hidden from civilization for centuries, perhaps millennia. But what had awaited those who had come before them?

It wasn't long before they found the first signs.

As the men followed a narrow path winding through the thick undergrowth, one of the sailors called out from ahead, his voice tight with fear. "Captain! Come quickly!"

Niño and Columbus rushed forward, their hearts pounding. When they reached the source of the cry, they stopped short, their breath catching in their throats. Lying scattered across the ground were bones—human bones, bleached white by time and the elements. Some were half-buried in the earth, while others lay exposed, twisted in unnatural positions. Tattered remnants of clothing clung to the remains, and rusted weapons and tools were strewn about.

The men stood in stunned silence, staring at the grisly sight. It was clear that these were not natives of the island. These were the bones of explorers, men like themselves, who had set out to uncover the secrets of the sea and had never returned.

"This..." Columbus whispered, his voice filled with shock. "This is the fate of those who came before us."

Niño knelt beside one of the skeletons, carefully examining the remnants of its clothing. The fabric, though rotted and worn, bore a design familiar to him—a European pattern, likely Spanish or Portuguese, from years past. These men had come from the same world as they had, but they had never made it back to tell their tale.

As the crew began to search the area, they uncovered more grim evidence of the lost expedition. Rusted swords, broken muskets, shattered pieces of navigational equipment—all signs of men who had fought, struggled, and died on this strange, forgotten island.

Columbus moved slowly through the scene, his eyes scanning the remains. His expression, usually so controlled and confident, had grown dark with realization. "We're not the first," he said quietly. "Others have tried to reach this place. And they failed."

One of the sailors picked up a rusted metal chest, its hinges creaking as he pried it open. Inside, wrapped in decaying parchment, were the remains of old maps and journals—records of a journey that had come to a tragic end. Niño took one of the journals carefully in his hands, the pages brittle and yellowed with age.

As he flipped through the crumbling book, the words written within were barely legible, but the story they told was all too familiar. The handwriting spoke of a captain who had led his crew across the ocean in search of new lands, just as Columbus had. The expedition had been filled with hope and ambition, but as the pages progressed, the tone shifted. The entries became more frantic, more desperate, as they encountered strange and terrifying forces—sea monsters, mysterious storms, and the haunting pull of the ocean's depths.

"It's the same," Niño murmured as he read. "They faced the same things we did. The same monsters, the same maelstrom. They were trying to reach the same place..."

"And they didn't make it," Columbus finished grimly.

The journal's final pages were filled with disjointed scribbles, barely coherent, as if the writer had been on the edge of madness. It spoke of something even more horrifying—a force within the island itself, something ancient and malevolent that had consumed the men's minds. The last entry ended abruptly, as though the writer had been cut off in the middle of his thoughts.

"God have mercy," one of the sailors whispered, his face pale as he looked around at the scattered remains. "These men... they were trapped here, just like we are. No one ever came to find them."

Niño closed the journal, his mind racing. The lost souls of the sea, the men who had come before them, had been forgotten by history. Their bones lay here, a grim testament to the dangers of venturing too far into the unknown. But what had killed them? Was it the island itself? Or something far more sinister, lurking just beneath the surface?

"We need to be careful," Niño said, rising to his feet. "Whatever happened to them—it's not over. This place... it's not what it seems."

Columbus nodded, his expression hardening. "We're not going to end up like them," he said firmly. "We've come too far to turn back now. We will survive this."

But even as he spoke, the men around them were growing more uneasy. The discovery of the remains had shaken their already fragile morale, and whispers of curses and ancient evils began to spread among the crew. They had survived the maelstrom, the Kraken, and the strange forces of the sea, but now, standing among the bones of those who had failed before them, they realized just how precarious their situation was.

Niño could feel the weight of their journey pressing down on him—the knowledge that they were walking the same path as those who had vanished, that they were facing the same dangers. And now, with the island looming around them, its strange flora and alien creatures watching from the shadows, he couldn't shake the feeling that they were being lured deeper into a trap.

As the men prepared to leave the site, Columbus ordered the journals and maps to be taken back to the ship. "We need to study these," he said. "There may be clues, something we can use to avoid their fate."

Niño nodded, though he wasn't sure what more they could learn from the doomed expedition. The path they were on was treacherous, but it was one they had to walk. The sea gods, the forces that ruled these waters and this land, were not done with them yet.

As they began to make their way back toward the ship, Niño paused, glancing back at the field of bones. The lost souls of the sea, forgotten by time, had left their warning. But it was up to them to heed it, or to suffer the same fate.

The island remained silent as they walked away, but Niño could still feel it—the quiet, watching presence, as if the land itself was waiting for the next chapter of their story to unfold.

Whatever lay ahead, they were no longer the first to face it. But they might be the last.

Chapter 27: The Ancient Ones

The discovery of the lost explorers had left the crew in a somber mood as they returned to the *Santa Maria*, their spirits heavy with the realization that they were not the first to venture into these mysterious waters. As the sun began to set, casting long shadows over the strange island, Columbus, Niño, and a select few from the crew gathered around the ancient stone structure they had found earlier in the jungle. There was something about the carvings etched into the worn stone, something that Niño couldn't shake from his mind.

For hours, he had studied the strange symbols, his fingers tracing their intricate patterns. The symbols were old, far older than anything he had encountered before, yet somehow familiar. His ancestors had left him knowledge of this place—a land where the sea gods held dominion and where ancient powers had once ruled. And now, as he examined the carvings, a chilling realization began to take hold.

"These are not just stories," Niño murmured, his voice barely audible as he pieced together the meaning of the inscriptions. "These symbols—they tell of something far older than we imagined."

Columbus, standing beside him, leaned in closer. "What do they say?"

Niño took a deep breath and began to explain. "The carvings speak of a great civilization that once thrived on this island, long before our time. A people who lived in harmony with the sea gods, who built temples and monuments in their honor. But they were not alone. The sea itself was alive with creatures—monsters that the island's people revered as protectors, guardians of a hidden power buried deep within the earth."

"The Kraken?" one of the sailors asked nervously, glancing around as if expecting the massive beast to emerge from the jungle.

Niño shook his head. "Not just the Kraken. There were many creatures—each one serving a different purpose, each one bound to protect the secrets of this island."

Columbus frowned, his gaze drifting to the towering trees and the dense jungle that surrounded them. "And what happened to this civilization?"

Niño hesitated before continuing, his voice lower now, filled with dread. "The inscriptions tell of a time when the people of this island sought to wield the power of the sea gods for themselves. They dug deeper into the earth, hoping to harness the ancient force that lay beneath their land. But they went too far. They awoke something—a force beyond their control. The sea gods turned against them, and the monsters that once protected the island became their executioners."

He gestured toward the carvings, his expression grim. "This place was abandoned, forgotten. The civilization collapsed, its people lost to the depths of the sea, their temples and cities swallowed by the earth. The sea gods sealed away the power that had been unearthed, burying it beneath the island and leaving the monsters to guard it for all time."

Columbus was silent for a long moment, his mind racing as he absorbed Niño's words. "So, these sea monsters... they're not just random creatures. They were created—or controlled—to protect this island and its secrets."

Niño nodded. "Yes. And we've been stirring them from their slumber. First the Leviathan, then the Kraken—both of them were warnings. We're getting too close to something they don't want us to find."

One of the sailors, his face pale with fear, spoke up. "Then we need to leave. We need to get back to the ships and sail away from this cursed place."

Niño's expression darkened. "It's not that simple. The sea gods won't let us leave now. We've crossed into their domain, and we've awakened their guardians. The only way out is through."

Columbus, though visibly shaken by the revelations, squared his shoulders and faced Niño. "You said the people of this island were seeking a hidden power. What kind of power are we talking about?"

Niño stared at the carvings, his heart heavy with the weight of what he was about to say. "It's a force older than the sea gods themselves, something buried deep within the earth—something that should never be disturbed. The sea gods sealed it away for a reason, and if we get too close, we risk waking it."

Columbus narrowed his eyes. "And if we wake it?"

Niño's voice was grave. "If we wake it, we could unleash a power capable of destroying not just this island, but everything around it. The sea, the land, even time itself could be torn apart. The sea gods were once worshipped, but even they feared what lies beneath this place."

The men shifted uneasily, the implications of Niño's words sinking in. They had come to this island seeking discovery, hoping to find riches and glory. But now, it seemed that they were on the verge of unleashing something far more dangerous than they could have imagined.

Columbus, though clearly disturbed, was not ready to give up. "There must be a way to avoid this. If the sea gods sealed this power away, then there must be a way to ensure it stays buried. We just need to find out how."

Niño shook his head. "The problem is, we've already disturbed too much. The Kraken, the Leviathan—they are part of the island's defenses. If we push any further, we risk triggering whatever ancient curse lies beneath."

"But we don't even know what this power is," Columbus argued. "It could be the key to everything—the greatest discovery in the history of the world."

Niño met his gaze, his eyes hard. "Or it could be our doom."

The tension between them was palpable. Columbus, ever the explorer, was torn between his insatiable curiosity and the undeniable danger that now faced them. Niño, guided by the wisdom of his ancestors, knew the risks all too well. This was no longer about discovery—it was about survival.

Before Columbus could respond, the ground beneath their feet trembled. The men looked around in alarm as a deep rumble echoed through the jungle, shaking the trees and sending flocks of strange birds screeching into the sky. The ancient stone structure, half-covered in moss and vines, groaned as cracks began to appear in its surface.

"We need to move," Niño said urgently, his eyes scanning the jungle. "Something's happening. The island is reacting to us."

Columbus nodded, his face pale. "Back to the ship. Now."

The men quickly gathered their supplies and began to make their way back through the dense foliage, their hearts pounding with the knowledge that the island was alive, watching their every move. As they hurried along the path, Niño's thoughts raced. The ancient force buried beneath the island was stirring, and the sea gods were growing restless.

The inscriptions had warned them, but it might already be too late.

As they reached the shore and prepared to return to the *Santa Maria*, Niño paused, turning back to the island one last time. The towering cliffs and twisted trees loomed ominously in the distance, and for a moment, he thought he saw something moving just beyond the edge of the jungle—something massive, watching from the shadows.

The Ancient Ones, the sea gods, had protected this island for eons, guarding the secrets of a forgotten civilization. But now, with each step they took, Niño feared they were drawing closer to a power that should never be awoken.

And if they did, there would be no escaping the wrath of the gods.

Chapter 28: The Temple of the Abyss

The *Santa Maria* lay anchored in the shallow waters off the strange, uncharted island, her once-mighty hull now battered and worn by the trials of the sea. The crew, exhausted and shaken, had spent the night in uneasy sleep, haunted by dreams of monstrous sea creatures and ancient gods. But with the rising sun came a new sense of determination, even if it was tinged with dread.

Niño stood on the deck, staring toward the dense jungle that concealed the island's secrets. The ancient inscriptions he had deciphered the day before were still fresh in his mind, their warnings clear: this island was no ordinary place. It held something ancient, something powerful, buried deep beneath its surface. And now, with the rumbling of the earth still fresh in his memory, Niño feared that they were closer to awakening that power than they realized.

As the crew prepared to venture inland once more, Columbus approached Niño, his expression set in a mask of grim resolve. "We need to move quickly," he said. "If there's any hope of making sense of this place, we need to understand what's hidden here."

Niño nodded, though his heart was heavy with caution. "I understand, Admiral. But the island is reacting to us. The deeper we go, the more dangerous it becomes."

Columbus placed a hand on Niño's shoulder, his voice low. "We've come too far to turn back now. Whatever power is hidden here, we need to know what it is. This could be the discovery of a lifetime."

Niño didn't argue further. He knew Columbus too well—the man's ambition and curiosity were unstoppable forces. But Niño also knew that their journey was no longer about glory. It was about survival, and the island had made it clear that they were intruding on something far older than themselves.

The group, led by Niño and Columbus, ventured back into the jungle, following the path they had taken the day before. The strange flora and fauna watched them silently from the shadows, and the air was thick with an unnatural stillness. As they walked, the ground beneath them seemed to hum with a quiet energy, as if the island itself was alive and aware of their presence.

After several hours of trekking through the dense foliage, the group came upon a clearing. And there, nestled between towering cliffs, was a sight that stopped them all in their tracks.

An ancient temple rose before them, half-buried in the earth and covered in thick vines and moss. The structure was massive, built of dark stone that seemed to absorb the light around it. Its walls were adorned with strange symbols and carvings, the same ones Niño had seen on the stone structure near the beach. But there was something different about this temple—something that made it feel more menacing, more alive.

The air around the temple seemed to vibrate with power. The closer they got, the heavier the air became, as if some invisible force was pressing down on them, warning them to stay away. The sailors muttered nervously to one another, their hands gripping their weapons as they eyed the temple with a mixture of awe and fear.

"This is it," Columbus said quietly, his eyes wide with wonder. "This is what we've been searching for."

Niño stepped forward, his gaze fixed on the temple's entrance. The doorway was dark, an open maw that seemed to beckon them inside. But as he studied the carvings around the entrance, his stomach tightened with dread.

"Admiral," Niño said slowly, his voice filled with unease, "this temple... it's not just a relic of the past. It's a tomb, a place where something was sealed away. The inscriptions here are different from the others. They warn of a power hidden within, a force that was never meant to be disturbed."

Columbus frowned, glancing at the carvings Niño had pointed out. "What do they say?"

Niño's hand traced the symbols etched into the stone. "They speak of the Abyss, the place where the sea gods buried a great and terrible force—a power that could bring ruin to the world above if unleashed. This temple was built to keep that force contained."

The crew exchanged uneasy glances, and one of the sailors, his voice trembling, muttered, "We shouldn't be here. We've seen what this island can do. The monsters, the storms—they're all trying to keep us away from this place."

Columbus turned to Niño, his expression hard. "You're saying this power is still here? Buried inside the temple?"

Niño nodded. "Yes. And if we disturb it, we could unleash something far worse than anything we've seen so far. The Kraken, the Leviathan—they were guardians, trying to protect this island's secrets. This temple... it's the heart of the island's power."

Columbus stood silently for a moment, his eyes locked on the dark entrance to the temple. His ambition burned brightly, but so did his fear. He had led his men through the horrors of the sea, faced down monsters and forces he couldn't explain, all in the name of discovery. But now, standing before the Temple of the Abyss, he could feel the weight of what they were about to awaken.

"We came here for answers," Columbus said at last, his voice firm. "If there's power in this place, we need to understand it. We can't turn back now."

Niño shook his head, his heart pounding. "Admiral, this is different. The island has been warning us from the beginning. If we step inside that temple, we could be walking into a trap we won't survive."

Columbus met Niño's gaze, his jaw set. "If we don't go in, we'll never know what's been hidden here. We've already stirred the island's guardians, Niño. It's too late to turn back."

The men stood in tense silence, the jungle around them strangely quiet. The temple loomed before them, its dark entrance a yawning void that seemed to radiate ancient power. Niño could feel the pull of the Abyss, the temptation to uncover the truth of what lay within. But he also knew the price of that knowledge could be far greater than they could afford.

One of the sailors, his face pale, stepped forward hesitantly. "Captain, with all due respect... maybe Niño's right. We've lost so much already. This place—it's cursed. We should leave while we still can."

Columbus turned to the sailor, his eyes cold. "If we leave now, we leave empty-handed. We came here for discovery, for knowledge. We can't abandon that now, not when we're so close."

Niño's voice was soft but firm as he spoke again. "Sometimes, there are things better left unknown."

The crew was divided. Some, driven by fear, wanted to leave the island and escape the curse they had brought upon themselves. Others, led by Columbus's unyielding ambition, felt that this was their moment, their chance to uncover the greatest secret the world had ever known.

Finally, Columbus turned back to Niño, his expression unreadable. "We go in," he said quietly. "But we proceed carefully. We take only what we need to understand this place—and then we leave."

Niño hesitated but eventually nodded. He knew there was no stopping Columbus now. The pull of the temple, the lure of the ancient power sealed inside, was too strong. But Niño couldn't shake the feeling that once they crossed the threshold, there would be no turning back.

As the men prepared to enter the temple, Niño felt the weight of his ancestors' warnings pressing heavily on his soul. The sea gods had buried something here, something that had the power to destroy worlds. And now, with every step they took toward the heart of the temple, they were drawing closer to awakening that power.

The Temple of the Abyss waited silently, its secrets locked away for centuries.

But not for much longer.

Chapter 29: The Sea Goddess

The entrance to the Temple of the Abyss loomed like a dark void, cold air seeping from its depths as if the earth itself breathed. The crew hesitated at the threshold, their faces pale with fear and uncertainty, their hearts torn between the lure of discovery and the terror of what might lie within. Niño stood at the front, his instincts screaming at him to turn back, to heed the warnings of the inscriptions and the ancient legends passed down by his ancestors.

But before they could move any closer, something strange happened.

A sudden gust of wind whipped through the jungle, carrying with it the scent of saltwater and the roar of distant waves. The men froze, their eyes widening as the ground beneath them trembled. The temple, the jungle, the very island itself seemed to hum with life, as if it were awakening from a long slumber. The air grew thick with an unearthly presence, and then, from the shadows at the edge of the clearing, something began to take shape.

A figure emerged, shimmering like the surface of the sea under the light of the moon. She was tall and otherworldly, her skin glowing with a pale, silvery hue that shifted like the waves. Her hair cascaded down her back in long, flowing tendrils, dark as the depths of the ocean and threaded with strands of light, like bioluminescence in the deepest waters. Her eyes, deep and ancient, gleamed with a power that seemed to reach beyond the confines of the world.

The crew gasped in awe, dropping to their knees instinctively, as though they were in the presence of a goddess. And in that moment, Niño knew exactly who—*what*—she was.

The Sea Goddess.

The air around her rippled with power as she stepped forward, her movements graceful and fluid, as though she were gliding through water rather than walking on land. She did not speak at first, but her gaze rested on Niño, her eyes locking with his in a way that made his heart pound in his chest.

"Who are you?" Columbus whispered, his voice trembling.

The Sea Goddess turned her gaze toward him, her expression both kind and formidable. When she spoke, her voice was like the crashing of waves, both soothing and commanding. "I am a guardian of the seas, of the realms that lie beyond the knowledge of men. I have watched over these waters since before your kind first set sail. You have ventured far, too far into the heart of my domain."

The men remained silent, too awestruck to speak, but Columbus, ever ambitious, took a step forward. "We came seeking knowledge, a new world. We only want to—"

The Sea Goddess raised her hand, and the very air around them seemed to still. "You seek what you cannot comprehend, mortal. The power that lies within this temple is not for you. It was sealed here long ago, buried by those who understood the dangers of awakening such forces."

She turned her gaze back to Niño, her eyes softening slightly. "You, Niño, son of the ancient navigators, you know the truth of this place. You have seen the warnings, and you understand what is at stake."

Niño's mouth went dry, but he managed to nod. "We didn't mean to disturb it. But we've come too far to turn back now. If we leave, we risk angering the sea gods even more."

The Sea Goddess studied him for a long moment before speaking again, her voice gentler. "You are not like the others who came before you. Those who sought to harness the power of the Abyss were consumed by their greed and ambition. But you, Niño, are different. You have the wisdom of your ancestors. You understand the balance that must be maintained."

The ground trembled once more, as if in warning. "The sea gods do not take kindly to those who trespass in their domain," the goddess continued. "But I can offer you a way out. Safe passage back to your world. But it will come at a price."

Columbus stepped forward again, his eyes wide with anticipation. "Anything! We'll give you anything—gold, treasure, whatever you desire!"

The Sea Goddess turned her gaze toward him, her expression cold. "I do not desire your gold or your treasures. What I demand is silence. If I grant you safe passage from this place, you must vow never to speak of what you have seen here. The world must never know of the ancient power that lies within these waters. If it is disturbed, it will bring ruin to the seas, to the land, to everything you hold dear."

Niño felt the weight of her words pressing down on him. He knew the truth of what she said—if the world learned of the power hidden in the Temple of the Abyss, it would be exploited, twisted for personal gain, and unleashed upon the world. The sea monsters, the Leviathan, the Kraken—they were not merely obstacles. They were guardians, protecting the world from the force that lay beneath the island. And if that force was awoken, no one would be able to stop it.

"Do you agree?" the Sea Goddess asked, her gaze sweeping over the crew.

Niño stepped forward, speaking for the first time with firm resolve. "I agree. We will take your offer. We'll leave this place and never speak of what we've seen."

Columbus opened his mouth to argue, but the look in Niño's eyes stopped him. He had seen enough. He knew that pushing any further would mean their end.

The Sea Goddess nodded, satisfied with Niño's answer. "Then it is done."

She raised her hands, and the air around them seemed to shimmer. A deep, rumbling sound echoed from the earth, and the ground beneath the temple trembled once more, but this time it began to calm. The pressure that had been building in the air dissipated, and the energy that had threatened to burst from the island's depths slowly receded.

"The path back will be clear," she said. "But remember this: if you ever return, if you ever speak of what you have found, the sea will rise against you. And no man, no ship, no empire will survive its wrath."

Niño nodded, his heart heavy with the weight of the vow they had made. He knew the danger they had narrowly avoided, and the responsibility that now rested on his shoulders. He turned to the crew, seeing the fear and relief in their faces.

The Sea Goddess gave one final glance to Niño, her expression unreadable. "Go now, while the seas remain calm. And may the gods show you mercy for your trespass."

With that, she dissolved into the shimmering air, fading back into the island as though she had never been there. The jungle around them seemed to exhale, the oppressive atmosphere lifting, replaced by a strange and peaceful stillness.

Niño turned to Columbus, who stood in stunned silence. "We leave now," Niño said quietly, but firmly. "We've been given a chance. Let's take it and go."

Columbus, though clearly reluctant to leave behind the mysteries of the island, nodded slowly. "We leave."

And so, the crew of the *Santa Maria* began their retreat, leaving behind the Temple of the Abyss, the ancient power sealed within, and the gods who had protected it for millennia. They had survived the monsters of the sea, the wrath of the ocean, and the horrors of the unknown—but their greatest challenge would be keeping the secret of the hidden world they had found.

As they boarded the ship and prepared to sail back into familiar waters, Niño glanced back at the island one last time. The Sea Goddess's warning echoed in his mind.

Some secrets, he knew, were meant to stay buried.

Part VII: Return to the Known World
Chapter 30: The Blood Oath

The *Santa Maria* swayed gently in the calm waters off the coast of the strange island as the crew gathered on deck, their faces tense and filled with a mixture of relief and fear. The encounter with the Sea Goddess still weighed heavily on their minds. They had been given a rare chance—a promise of safe passage home—but it came with a price that left many unsettled. The goddess's warning echoed in Niño's mind, and he knew that their survival depended on their ability to honor the vow they had made.

Columbus stood at the helm, his jaw clenched as he stared out at the horizon, the island now a distant shadow behind them. He had always been a man of ambition, driven by the need for discovery and glory. But the weight of the Sea Goddess's words had shaken even him. He had seen the power that lay hidden within the island, the monsters that guarded it, and the ancient force that should never be disturbed.

"We made a pact," Niño reminded him quietly, standing by his side. "The goddess gave us a chance to leave with our lives, but we must honor our vow."

Columbus nodded, though his expression was hard. "I know, Niño. We will keep our silence."

But as the ship sailed away from the island, it became clear that not everyone aboard shared Columbus and Niño's resolve. Whispers had begun to spread among the crew, rumors of treasure, power, and glory hidden within the temple. Some of the men, their minds still clouded by greed and ambition, had not been satisfied with the Sea Goddess's offer. To them, the thought of returning to Spain empty-handed, with nothing to show for their perilous journey, was unbearable.

One evening, as the ship glided through calm waters, Niño overheard a heated conversation among a group of sailors below deck. He crept closer, listening intently as the voices grew louder.

"We came all this way, fought through storms, monsters, and gods," one of the sailors, a man named Garcia, muttered angrily. "And for what? To return with nothing? No one back home will believe us, and even if they do, we'll be laughed at for turning away from riches like cowards."

Another sailor, a stocky man named Luis, nodded in agreement. "Garcia's right. There's more to that island than just danger. We saw the temple—it's ancient, filled with secrets that could make us rich beyond our wildest dreams. Columbus and Niño want to run, but we shouldn't be so quick to throw away our chance at fortune."

Niño's heart sank as he listened. He had feared this. The Sea Goddess's warning had been clear—if they broke the vow, the wrath of the sea gods would fall upon them. But these men were willing to risk everything for the chance at glory.

Garcia's voice grew darker. "We don't need everyone to go back. A small group of us could return to the island, sneak into the temple, and claim what's inside. By the time Columbus realizes we're gone, we'll be back with more than enough to buy our freedom."

Luis grinned, his eyes gleaming with greed. "We could rule Spain with what's in that temple. They say the gods buried their treasures there—who knows what we'll find?"

Niño knew he had to act. He couldn't allow these men to return to the island and break the pact, or they would doom not just themselves, but everyone aboard. He quietly retreated to the deck and sought out Columbus, his mind racing with the gravity of the situation.

"Admiral," Niño said urgently as he approached Columbus. "There's a group of men below deck—they're planning to defy the goddess's warning. They want to return to the island, to the temple."

Columbus's eyes flashed with anger. "Fools! Don't they understand what's at stake?"

"They're blinded by greed," Niño replied grimly. "They think they can claim the temple's secrets and escape the goddess's wrath."

Columbus clenched his fists. "We made a blood oath to the Sea Goddess, Niño. We vowed never to reveal what we found, never to disturb the island again. If they break that oath, the gods will destroy us all."

Without hesitation, Columbus and Niño descended below deck to confront the dissenting sailors. As they reached the group, Garcia and Luis were in the middle of convincing a few more men to join their cause, their words dripping with promises of wealth and power.

"You will do no such thing," Columbus's voice cut through the air like a blade, startling the men.

The sailors turned, their expressions shifting from surprise to defiance. Garcia stepped forward, his eyes cold. "Why shouldn't we? You've led us through hell, Captain. You've made us face monsters, storms, and death, and now you want us to walk away with nothing? There's treasure on that island, and we have every right to claim it."

Columbus glared at him. "You don't understand the forces you're dealing with. The Sea Goddess has offered us mercy, but only if we honor our vow. If you return to the island, if you disturb the temple, you'll doom us all."

Luis sneered. "We've already survived more than most men could dream of. Why should we fear a goddess's threat? What's she going to do? Send more monsters? We'll be ready."

Niño stepped forward, his voice steady. "You won't survive another attack. The monsters we faced were nothing compared to the power that lies beneath the temple. The Sea Goddess herself warned us—if we break our oath, we'll awaken something far worse."

But Garcia was unmoved. "That's a risk I'm willing to take. If you don't have the stomach for it, Niño, step aside."

Columbus's hand went to the hilt of his sword, his voice cold. "You would risk the lives of everyone aboard this ship for your greed? If you defy me, you will not live to return to that island."

Tension crackled in the air as the sailors stared at Columbus, their defiance slowly turning to fear. They had seen the horrors of the sea, the monsters that lurked beneath the waves, and the power that had nearly destroyed them. But even in the face of such danger, greed still burned in their hearts.

For a long moment, no one moved.

Then, in a sudden burst of rage, Garcia lunged at Columbus, drawing a knife. But Columbus was faster, drawing his sword and parrying the attack with a swift, practiced motion. In an instant, the ship erupted into chaos as a brief scuffle broke out between the loyal crew and the dissenters.

It was over quickly. Garcia and Luis were subdued, their rebellion quashed before it could gain any more traction. The other sailors, cowed by the sight of their leaders' defeat, offered no resistance.

Breathing heavily, Columbus sheathed his sword and addressed the men. "You will not break the oath. You will not return to the island. If you do, the Sea Goddess's wrath will fall upon us all, and none of us will survive. Do you understand?"

The men, shaken and pale, nodded in fear. The blood oath they had sworn was not just a promise—it was a matter of life and death.

That night, as the *Santa Maria* continued its voyage home, Niño stood at the rail, staring out at the endless sea. The island was far behind them now, but the weight of what they had discovered still pressed heavily on his heart. The power they had left behind in the Temple of the Abyss was a secret too dangerous for the world to know, and their survival now hinged on their silence.

Columbus approached him, his expression solemn. "We've averted disaster for now, but I fear the temptations of what we found will haunt us forever."

Niño nodded. "The Sea Goddess will be watching. If anyone speaks of what we've seen, she will come for us."

They stood in silence for a moment, the sea stretching endlessly before them. The men who had defied the pact had been dealt with, but Niño knew that greed and ambition were forces that could never truly be silenced. The world would always seek out power, and the secrets of the island would remain a dangerous lure.

But for now, they had escaped. The blood oath held, and the gods had granted them mercy.

All they had to do was keep their silence.

And pray that no one else would ever find the hidden island, or the ruin that lay buried beneath its surface.

Chapter 31: The Final Storm

The *Santa Maria* and the remaining ships had set their course for home, the uncharted island now a distant shadow behind them. Though the Sea Goddess had granted them safe passage, there was an uneasy tension that gripped the crew. The pact had been made, the blood oath sworn, but Niño knew the goddess's mercy was not infinite. There were still whispers among the men—quiet, dangerous murmurs of defiance and greed. The rebellion led by Garcia and Luis had been crushed, but not all hearts aboard the ships had fully accepted the gravity of their vow.

The skies were deceptively calm as the fleet sailed through the open waters, but Niño could feel something was wrong. The air was thick, heavy with a strange stillness, and the horizon, though clear, seemed to ripple with an unseen energy. He stood at the helm, his eyes scanning the endless sea as the crew moved about their duties with quiet unease.

Columbus approached, his expression grim. "We should have been further from the island by now," he muttered. "The winds have been uncooperative, and the sea is too calm. It feels like we're being... watched."

Niño nodded. He had felt the same oppressive presence since they left the island. The Sea Goddess had warned them—any act of defiance, any breach of their oath, would bring destruction. And while they had dealt with the most vocal dissenters, Niño couldn't shake the feeling that something had been set in motion, something they could no longer control.

As the day wore on, the stillness became unbearable. The sails hung limp in the lack of wind, and the sea, once a friend to their journey, had become like glass, reflecting the darkening sky above. The crew grew more anxious, their eyes darting to the horizon as if expecting a storm to descend at any moment.

Then, in the late afternoon, the winds changed.

A single gust swept across the deck, followed by another, stronger, more forceful. The sails filled suddenly, and the ship lurched forward as if something was pulling it across the water. The sky, once clear, began to darken rapidly, swirling clouds forming overhead, casting the sea in shadow. The temperature dropped, and the wind howled through the rigging, sending shivers down the spines of the men.

"It's her," Niño said under his breath, his heart pounding. "The goddess is angry."

Before Columbus could respond, a loud crack of thunder split the air, and the sky opened up in a torrent of rain. The once-calm sea erupted into chaos, waves rising and crashing against the sides of the ships with terrifying force. Lightning streaked across the sky, illuminating the dark clouds that now swirled in a massive spiral above them—an unnatural storm, summoned by the wrath of the Sea Goddess herself.

"Brace yourselves!" Columbus shouted over the roar of the wind, but the men were already scrambling to secure the sails and tie down the rigging.

The *Santa Maria* groaned under the strain as the waves grew larger, crashing over the deck and sending torrents of seawater across the ship. The other ships in the fleet, the *Niña* and the *Pinta*, struggled to keep pace, their crews battling against the violent winds and surging waves. The storm was unlike anything they had encountered—a force of nature that seemed bent on tearing them apart.

Niño gripped the helm tightly, fighting to keep the ship on course. But even as he did, he could feel the storm closing in around them, the air thick with the Sea Goddess's fury. This was no ordinary storm. It was punishment—a final reckoning for the disobedience that still lingered among the crew.

"Look!" one of the sailors screamed, pointing toward the horizon.

Through the sheets of rain and crashing waves, they saw it: the *Pinta*, caught in the heart of the storm. Its sails were torn, and the ship pitched dangerously as a massive wave towered over it, ready to consume it whole. The men aboard screamed in terror as the wave crashed down, smashing the ship with a deafening roar.

The *Pinta* was lost in an instant, swallowed by the sea.

Niño's heart sank as he watched the ship disappear beneath the waves. The storm, merciless and unrelenting, had claimed its first victim. And still, the winds howled, and the waves raged on, as if the Sea Goddess would not be satisfied until they were all dragged into the depths.

Columbus stood frozen, his face pale with shock as the reality of their situation set in. "We have to get out of this storm," he shouted to Niño, his voice barely audible over the thunder. "If we stay here, we're finished!"

Niño nodded, his hands trembling as he struggled to keep the *Santa Maria* steady. The ship was battered and worn, the sails torn, and the hull creaked under the weight of the storm. But he knew there was no escaping the Sea Goddess's wrath. This storm was not natural—it was a punishment, unleashed because someone among them had broken the vow.

Another bolt of lightning split the sky, illuminating the deck for a brief moment. And in that flash of light, Niño saw it—one of the sailors, crouched near the cargo hold, clutching something in his hands. Something glinting in the light.

Gold.

Niño's heart raced as he realized what had happened. Despite their promises, despite the blood oath, one of the men had stolen from the temple. They had taken something from the island, and now the Sea Goddess was exacting her vengeance.

Without hesitation, Niño ran toward the sailor, who was frantically trying to hide the stolen treasure. "What have you done?" Niño shouted, his voice filled with anger and fear. "You broke the oath!"

The sailor, his face twisted with panic, looked up at Niño, clutching the gold like a lifeline. "I thought— I thought it wouldn't matter. Just a small piece, just—"

Before he could finish, a massive wave crashed over the deck, knocking them both off their feet. Niño scrambled to his feet, but the sailor was gone, swept into the churning sea, the stolen treasure vanishing with him.

The storm raged on, but in that moment, Niño felt the tide shift. The winds, though still violent, seemed to ease slightly, and the waves no longer towered as high. The Sea Goddess had claimed her justice.

Niño staggered back to the helm, drenched and exhausted, his heart heavy with the weight of what had just happened. The price of disobedience had been paid in blood, but at what cost?

As the storm slowly began to subside, Columbus joined him at the helm, his face grim. "Is it over?"

Niño nodded, though his eyes remained fixed on the horizon. "For now. But the goddess's warning still stands. If we ever speak of this place, if we ever return, she will destroy us all."

Columbus looked out at the sea, where the wreckage of the *Pinta* had vanished beneath the waves. "We won't forget."

The storm, now fading into the distance, had left its mark on the crew. They had witnessed the power of the gods, the fury of the sea, and the price of betrayal. The journey home would be long, but Niño knew that the greatest challenge lay not in the sea ahead, but in keeping the vow they had made.

As the *Santa Maria* sailed on, Niño whispered a silent prayer to the Sea Goddess, hoping that their sacrifice would be enough to earn her mercy.

And that no one would ever again dare to defy the will of the sea.

Chapter 32: The Navigator's Sacrifice

The storm had passed, leaving the *Santa Maria* limping through the calm seas, battered but still afloat. The destruction of the *Pinta* and the disappearance of the rebellious sailor who had broken the oath weighed heavily on the crew. The men worked in silence, their faces pale and their hearts heavy with the knowledge that they had come perilously close to losing everything. The Sea Goddess's wrath had been unleashed, and though the storm had subsided, Niño knew that the danger was far from over.

The air felt different now—heavy, charged with an unspoken tension that seemed to hang over the ship like a dark cloud. The men moved quietly, avoiding each other's eyes, as if afraid that speaking too loudly might invite the sea gods' fury once more. Even Columbus, who had always been full of bold ambition, seemed subdued, his face drawn and tired as he stood at the helm, staring out at the vast, empty ocean.

Niño could feel it too. The gods were not yet satisfied. The stolen gold had been returned to the sea, but the violation of their pact still lingered in the air like a curse. Something more was needed, something to fully appease the sea gods and ensure the survival of the remaining crew and ships.

And Niño knew what it was.

He had been thinking about it since the storm had begun to fade, the realization settling over him with a heavy certainty. The sea gods had spared them, but they had demanded a price for their mercy. The pact they had made was not just a vow of silence, but a promise—a blood oath that required a personal sacrifice to balance the scales.

Niño had always known his connection to the sea was different. His ancestors, the ancient navigators, had passed down their knowledge of the oceans and the gods who ruled them. He had understood the warnings, the signs, the subtle messages from the sea. And now, it was clear to him that his own bloodline carried the weight of that ancient knowledge, and with it, the responsibility to protect those who traveled these dangerous waters.

Standing at the bow of the ship, Niño watched the sun sink lower on the horizon, the golden light shimmering on the surface of the water. The calm sea stretched out endlessly before them, but beneath that serene surface, he could feel the restless presence of the gods, waiting for the final payment to be made.

He took a deep breath and made his decision.

That evening, as the crew prepared for the night, Niño approached Columbus, his expression solemn. The men around them were weary, their bodies bruised and battered, their minds filled with fear. But Niño had no fear left in him. He had made peace with what needed to be done.

"Admiral," Niño said quietly, his voice steady, "I need to speak with you."

Columbus looked up from his maps, his brow furrowed in concern. He had grown to trust Niño deeply throughout their journey, relying on his wisdom and knowledge to guide them through the darkest moments of their voyage. And now, seeing the seriousness in Niño's eyes, Columbus knew that something important was about to be said.

"What is it?" Columbus asked, setting the maps aside.

Niño took a deep breath, his hands clasped in front of him. "The sea gods are still watching us. They haven't fully forgiven us for breaking the oath. The storm was a warning, and the loss of the *Pinta* was their first act of judgment. But they require something more."

Columbus's eyes darkened. "What more could they want? We've lost men. We've lost a ship. We've upheld the vow."

Niño shook his head. "It's not enough. The sea gods demand a personal sacrifice—something to ensure the survival of the rest of the crew, and to seal the pact we made. If we don't offer it willingly, I fear they will take everything."

Columbus's face paled as the full weight of Niño's words sank in. "A sacrifice?"

Niño nodded. "Yes. And it must be me."

Columbus stared at him in shock, his mind reeling. "No. Absolutely not. You've been our guide, our protector. You've led us through every trial. I won't let you do this."

But Niño was resolute. He had already made his decision, and there was no turning back. "I am the navigator. The one who carries the bloodline of the ancient navigators who first understood the sea gods' power. It is my responsibility to ensure that this crew returns home safely. The gods spared us for a reason, but they are waiting for this final act of appeasement. Without it, none of us will survive."

Columbus shook his head, his voice filled with desperation. "There must be another way. We can find something else to offer—something other than your life."

Niño placed a hand on Columbus's shoulder, his gaze steady. "There is no other way. I have felt it in my bones, in the whispers of the sea. This is the only way to ensure that the men make it back to Spain. This is my destiny, Admiral."

Columbus stood frozen, his mind torn between his loyalty to Niño and the reality of what he was being asked to accept. He had led the men through storms, through monsters, through unimaginable horrors, but this—this was a sacrifice he had never anticipated.

"I'll return to the sea," Niño said softly. "The sea gods will take me, and in exchange, they will let the rest of you go. The storm will not return, and you'll have calm waters all the way home."

Tears welled in Columbus's eyes, but he knew there was no stopping Niño. He had seen the truth in the goddess's warning and understood the nature of the pact they had made.

Niño stepped back, his resolve unshakable. "I will go alone. Tell the men nothing. Let them believe that I've simply gone overboard in the night. It will be easier for them that way."

Columbus swallowed hard, his voice breaking. "You're a better man than any of us, Niño."

Niño smiled faintly, though there was sadness in his eyes. "I've just been following the sea's call."

Without another word, Niño turned and made his way to the bow of the ship, where the moonlight shimmered on the dark waters below. The sea stretched out before him, vast and mysterious, and as he looked out at the horizon, he felt a deep peace settle over him. This was where he belonged—in the embrace of the ocean, where the gods ruled and the ancient powers slumbered.

With a final glance back at the ship, Niño climbed onto the railing and leapt into the sea.

The water closed over him silently, and for a moment, the world stood still.

As Niño sank into the depths, the sea seemed to come alive around him, the currents swirling with an otherworldly energy. He felt no fear, only a sense of acceptance, as if the gods themselves were welcoming him home.

And then, the currents grew calm.

The storm never returned. The seas remained still, and the winds steady, as the remaining ships sailed safely back to Spain.

Niño's sacrifice had been accepted, and the gods had kept their promise.

The navigator was gone, but his legacy lived on in the hearts of the men who returned. They had survived the monsters, the storms, and the wrath of the sea gods. And though they carried the weight of the secret they could never reveal, they knew that they owed their lives to the man who had given everything to protect them.

And so, the *Santa Maria* sailed on, guided by the memory of the man who had navigated their journey through the unknown.

The sea, at last, was at peace.

Chapter 33: The Long Journey Home

The *Santa Maria* drifted across the open ocean, her sails full of wind but her crew hollowed by exhaustion. The storm had passed, the wrath of the Sea Goddess appeased, and the island that had once loomed so large in their minds was now a distant memory, left far behind. Yet, the journey home—what should have been a relief after the horrors they had endured—felt like a cruel, drawn-out test of their endurance.

The ship was eerily quiet. The usual sounds of life at sea—the chatter of the men, the clatter of tools, the hum of work—had been replaced by a somber silence. The crew moved like ghosts, haunted by what they had seen, by the losses they had suffered, and by the sacrifice that had saved their lives. Niño's absence weighed heavily on everyone, though none spoke of it. Columbus had honored Niño's request, telling the men that the navigator had gone overboard in the night, lost to the sea. It was a half-truth, and though the men accepted it, they knew that something far greater had transpired.

Niño's sacrifice had ensured their survival, but it had also left an unshakable mark on the souls of those who remained.

As the days turned into weeks, the men began to feel the strain of their journey. Supplies were running low, and though the weather remained calm, the ship itself was damaged from the storm and the earlier battles with the sea creatures. The hull groaned with each wave, and the sails, patched and worn, struggled to maintain speed. Every creak of the ship was a reminder of how close they had come to destruction, and every glance at the horizon was filled with uncertainty.

Food and fresh water became scarce. What rations they had left were divided carefully among the crew, but it wasn't enough. Hunger gnawed at their stomachs, and thirst dried their throats. The men grew weaker with each passing day, their once-strong bodies now frail and gaunt. But it wasn't just the physical hardships that weighed on them—it was the memories, the constant replaying of the horrors they had faced on the island and at sea.

The sight of the Kraken's tentacles rising from the depths, the terrifying screech of the Leviathan, the whispers of the sea that had lured men to their deaths—these images haunted their sleep and followed them into their waking hours. The men spoke little, and when they did, it was in whispers, as if afraid that speaking too loudly might summon the gods back to claim them.

Columbus, though he had always been the pillar of strength and leadership, was not immune to the weight of the journey. He stood at the helm most days, staring out at the horizon with a look of deep contemplation. He had seen things no man should see, had survived trials that had broken even the strongest of his crew, and had lost the man who had been his most trusted guide.

As captain, it was his duty to lead them home, but Columbus felt the crushing guilt of those who hadn't survived—those who had perished in the storm, been taken by the sea monsters, or disappeared into the dark waters. And though he did not speak of it, the memory of Niño's sacrifice haunted him most of all.

One evening, as the sun dipped below the horizon and painted the sky in shades of orange and red, Columbus gathered the crew on deck. They stood silently, their faces gaunt and weathered, their eyes filled with the weight of their journey.

"We are close to home," Columbus began, his voice steady but laced with exhaustion. "But the sea has tested us, and it will continue to test us. We've lost many along the way, and their memory will remain with us always. But we are the ones who survived. We are the ones who will return to Spain."

The men listened in silence, their faces grim. They had heard speeches like this before, but this time it felt different. This time, the words carried the weight of finality.

"Niño gave everything to protect us," Columbus continued, his voice thick with emotion. "He knew the dangers of the sea gods, and he made the ultimate sacrifice to ensure that we would make it home. We owe him our lives."

The crew shifted uneasily, some bowing their heads in respect, others too drained to respond. The loss of Niño had affected them all, even those who had not known him well. He had been their guide, their protector, and without him, they felt adrift in more ways than one.

"We will honor his memory," Columbus said firmly. "But we must also honor the pact we made. The Sea Goddess granted us safe passage, but that safety is fragile. We must never speak of what we found on that island. We must never return to those cursed waters. Do you all understand?"

A murmur of agreement passed through the crew, though it was clear that some of the men still harbored thoughts of the treasure they had left behind. But the fear of the gods, and the memory of the storm that had nearly destroyed them, was enough to keep most of them silent.

As the days wore on, the hardships continued to pile up. More men fell ill from hunger and exhaustion, their bodies too weak to continue working. The ship's doctor did what he could with the limited supplies they had, but there were no miracles left to give. Death became an ever-present companion, stalking the ship as it slowly limped toward home.

The crew, broken and depleted, held on to what little hope they had left. They prayed for a sighting of land, for the familiar shores of Spain to rise up from the horizon and bring an end to their suffering. But the ocean stretched endlessly before them, an expanse of blue that offered no answers, no comfort.

It was Columbus who remained their anchor. Despite his own grief and exhaustion, he continued to lead, keeping the ship on course, tending to the needs of the men as best he could. But even he knew that their survival hung by a thread.

One night, as the ship drifted under a sky full of stars, Niño's absence felt more profound than ever. Columbus stood alone at the bow, gazing up at the constellations that had once guided them so faithfully. He thought of the navigator, the man who had understood the sea in ways Columbus never could. Niño had given his life to appease the gods, to ensure that the rest of them would make it home.

Now, with every wave that lapped against the ship, Columbus could almost feel Niño's presence, a quiet whisper in the wind, a guiding hand that seemed to push them forward through the darkness.

The journey home was not over. They still had miles to sail, still had hardships to endure. But as the stars twinkled above and the sea remained calm, Columbus allowed himself to believe that they would make it.

The gods had been appeased. Niño's sacrifice had not been in vain.

And somewhere, just beyond the horizon, home awaited.

Chapter 34: The Promise of Silence

The waters had finally calmed as the battered *Santa Maria* neared the shores of Spain. After weeks of hardship, hunger, and loss, the sight of land brought a collective sigh of relief from the crew. They had made it. But even as the promise of home lay just ahead, the men were haunted by the ghosts of their journey—the monsters they had fought, the island they had discovered, and the power they had left behind.

Columbus stood at the helm, staring at the distant coastline with a mixture of exhaustion and resolve. They had survived the wrath of the sea gods, had endured the storm and the trials of the voyage, but there was one final task to complete before they could truly return: the vow of silence. The blood oath they had made with the Sea Goddess could not be broken, for the consequences would be too dire. The promise to keep their journey secret had been made in desperation, but now, standing on the cusp of returning to the world they knew, the weight of that promise pressed heavily on their souls.

Niño, though gone, still felt present in every decision Columbus made. The navigator's sacrifice had saved them all, and it was his understanding of the sea gods that had guided them through the perilous waters. His absence was a reminder of the price they had paid, and Columbus knew he could never allow that sacrifice to be in vain.

As the ship slowly approached the harbor, Columbus called the remaining crew to the deck. The men, weary and broken, gathered around him in silence, their eyes heavy with the memories of their journey. They had lost many along the way, but those who had survived knew they were bound by a pact they could not break.

"We are almost home," Columbus began, his voice strong despite the fatigue that tugged at him. "But before we set foot on land, there is something we must all remember. The sea gods spared us, but only on the condition that we keep their secret. What we found, what we saw—none of it can ever be spoken of."

The men stood in silence, their faces grim. They knew the cost of disobedience. They had seen it firsthand in the destruction of the *Pinta* and the terrible storm that had nearly claimed them all.

"We swore an oath," Columbus continued. "An oath to the Sea Goddess herself. If we break that vow, if we reveal what we discovered on that island, the gods will punish us. They will not be merciful a second time."

One of the sailors, his voice hoarse, spoke up. "And what of the treasure? The gold? We were so close..."

Columbus shook his head. "Forget the treasure. Forget the island. The price of seeking it again is too high. If we return, if we disturb that power, none of us will survive. The sea gods made that clear."

The crew exchanged uneasy glances, but the memory of the storm still hung heavily over them, and the sight of the *Pinta* disappearing beneath the waves remained etched in their minds. They knew better than to question the will of the gods.

"We will say nothing," Columbus said firmly, his eyes scanning the faces of the men. "When we dock, we will tell the people of Spain that we explored new waters, but we found no new land. Our journey was long, but there were no riches, no new discoveries. We will bury the truth of this voyage, and it will die with us."

The crew nodded slowly, understanding the gravity of the situation. They had come so far, faced so many dangers, and now they were being asked to forget it all. But there was no other choice. They had survived because of the promise they made, and to break that promise would be to invite ruin.

As the crew dispersed, Columbus remained at the helm, watching the shoreline grow closer. The city of Palos de la Frontera was just ahead, and with it, the end of their harrowing journey. But even as they neared home, Columbus could not shake the feeling that their silence would not be enough. The island, the temple, the power they had left behind—it was still out there, waiting, and one day, someone might find it.

And when they did, the gods would not be so forgiving.

Later that evening, as the ship was moored in the harbor and preparations were made to disembark, Columbus found himself alone on the deck. The bustling sounds of the city below filled the air, but Columbus's mind was elsewhere. He thought of Niño—of the man who had guided them through the unknown, of his sacrifice, and of the knowledge he had taken with him to the sea.

Though Niño was gone, his spirit remained, a quiet presence in the back of Columbus's mind. The navigator had understood the dangers of the sea gods in ways no one else could, and it was that understanding that had saved them. But there was something else that lingered, something that had haunted Niño before his final act of sacrifice—unease. The feeling that by discovering the island, by setting foot in that temple, they had unleashed something far more dangerous than they realized.

The sea gods had been appeased, but Columbus knew they had not forgotten. The pact they had made was fragile, and though they had kept their side of the bargain, the power beneath the island was still there, waiting. Waiting for someone else to find it, waiting for another ship to stumble upon its shores.

Columbus stood at the bow, staring out at the dark horizon, where the sea stretched endlessly into the night. He had made a promise to keep the secret of their voyage, and he would honor that promise. But even as he swore to protect the world from the knowledge of the island, he couldn't help but feel a deep sense of unease.

The sea, with all its mysteries and dangers, was vast and unknowable. And somewhere, far beyond the reach of Spain, beyond the sight of any map, the hidden island still lay in wait, its power sealed beneath the surface, guarded by the ancient gods of the sea.

But for how long?

Columbus knew that, despite their vow of silence, the world would eventually change. Explorers would continue to sail, driven by ambition, greed, and the desire to discover what lay beyond the horizon. And one day, someone would return to the island. One day, the sea gods would be disturbed again.

And when that day came, Columbus feared that no one would be able to stop the fury that would follow.

With a heavy heart, he turned and walked back toward the cabin, the weight of their journey pressing down on him like an anchor. The promise of silence had been made, but the threat of the unknown still loomed.

As he disappeared into the shadows of the ship, the waves lapped quietly against the hull, whispering their eternal secrets.

And in the distance, the gods watched, waiting.

Chapter 35: Legends of the Sea

The *Santa Maria* had returned to Spain, battered and worn, but its crew alive. The docks of Palos de la Frontera buzzed with excitement at the sight of the returning ship, but the mood aboard was anything but celebratory. The men who disembarked were shadows of the sailors who had once set out with hopes of glory and discovery. Their gaunt faces, hollow eyes, and haunted expressions told of a voyage that had taken more than they could ever have imagined.

As they stepped onto solid ground, the weight of their silence hung between them like a fog. The world knew nothing of the horrors they had faced—of the sea monsters, the mysterious island, the wrath of the gods. To the people of Spain, they were returning from an ordinary expedition, with no new lands discovered and no treasures to offer. And that was how it would remain.

Columbus walked slowly down the gangplank, his mind still adrift in the memories of the voyage. His boots touched the familiar soil of his homeland, but there was no sense of victory, no sense of triumph. Only a deep and gnawing unease. Behind him, the crew moved quietly, their eyes downcast, the weight of the Sea Goddess's warning ever-present in their minds.

News of the *Santa Maria*'s return spread quickly, and soon, the harbor was filled with curious townspeople, merchants, and officials eager to hear tales of adventure. But Columbus and his men said little. They answered the questions with vague accounts of storms and misfortune, of empty waters and unexplored lands. The true story of their journey—of the island, the temple, and the sacrifice—remained locked in their hearts, bound by the blood oath they had sworn.

But not all were so easily satisfied with the quiet return. Whispers began to spread through the streets and taverns, carried by sailors and dockworkers who had overheard bits and pieces of the crew's mutterings. Tales of sea monsters, of a hidden island far beyond the known world, began to take root in the imaginations of the people. The stories grew wilder with each retelling: an island filled with unimaginable riches, guarded by creatures born of nightmares; a temple of gold buried beneath the ocean's depths; a place where the laws of nature no longer applied.

The rumors swirled through Spain like a tempest, igniting the imaginations of would-be explorers, merchants, and adventurers. The taverns of Seville and Barcelona buzzed with talk of the lost land, and maps of the Atlantic were pored over by those eager to find what Columbus had supposedly left behind. The legend of the hidden island became a fever dream of glory and fortune, a siren's call to those who sought to conquer the unknown.

Columbus, now back in his quarters, could hear the rumors spreading like wildfire. He sat at his desk, staring at a blank map of the Atlantic, his mind filled with conflicting emotions. The world was hungry for new lands, for discoveries that would bring wealth and power to the crown. But Columbus knew the truth. He had seen the island. He had felt the presence of the gods who guarded it, had witnessed their wrath. And he had lost men—good men—to the madness that came with seeking its secrets.

A knock on his door broke his reverie. One of his most trusted officers entered, his expression grim. "The rumors are spreading faster than we can control, Admiral. Every tavern, every market—people are talking of sea monsters and lost lands. They say you found something out there."

Columbus sighed deeply. "They're wrong," he said, though even he could hear the uncertainty in his voice. "We found nothing."

The officer hesitated. "But the men—they've been speaking of things. Strange things. Some of them are starting to question why we returned with so little to show."

Columbus's eyes darkened. "They will keep silent, as we agreed. They know what's at stake. The Sea Goddess will not be merciful if we betray the oath."

The officer nodded but lingered at the doorway. "And what of the others? The ones who are already planning new voyages to find this... hidden island?"

Columbus stood slowly, walking to the window that overlooked the harbor. In the distance, he could see the ships moored in the bay, their sails furled, ready for new expeditions. Spain was a nation of explorers, driven by the desire to conquer new lands, to find new worlds. It was only a matter of time before someone else ventured into the waters they had barely escaped from.

"They won't find it," Columbus said quietly, more to himself than to the officer. "The island... it's hidden for a reason. The gods won't allow it to be disturbed again."

But even as he said the words, a flicker of doubt crossed his mind. The island, the temple, the power they had left behind—it was still out there, waiting. And the Sea Goddess had made it clear: if anyone returned, if the pact was broken, there would be no escape from her wrath.

That evening, as Columbus sat alone in the fading light, the legends of the sea continued to grow. He could hear the distant clamor of voices in the streets, sailors spinning tales of the Kraken and the Leviathan, of the monstrous forces that lurked beneath the waves. The men of Spain had tasted the edges of the unknown, and now they hungered for more.

But Columbus, and those who had survived the journey, knew the truth: there were some places man was never meant to go, some secrets better left buried in the depths of the ocean. Niño's sacrifice had saved them, but it had also sealed their fate—they were now the keepers of a secret that could never be spoken.

As the moon rose high over the harbor, casting its pale light over the ships below, Columbus made one final vow. He would protect the world from the knowledge of the island, from the power that slumbered beneath its surface. He would ensure that the legend remained just that—a legend, a tale to entertain in taverns but never to be pursued.

But deep down, he knew that silence could only last so long. The sea was vast, and there would always be those who sought to explore its furthest reaches. One day, someone would find the island again.

And when they did, the Sea Goddess would be waiting.

For now, the legend of the hidden island and its monstrous guardians would remain just that—a story, a myth whispered among sailors and adventurers. But for Columbus, for Niño, and for the men who had survived, it was a reality they could never forget.

The sea, with all its mysteries, held its secrets tightly. And though the world would chase after them, the true cost of those secrets was known only to a few.

And those few would carry the burden of silence to their graves.

About the Author

David Moore is a seasoned author, known for his intricate suspense thrillers that delve into the murky world of conspiracies and high-stakes drama. With a background in freelance writing, David spent years writing about political scandals and global conflicts, experiences that now fuel his gripping narratives.

Milton Keynes UK
Ingram Content Group UK Ltd.
UKHW041822201024
449814UK00001B/77

9 798227 114020